SCANDAL (99 DADDIES BOOK 4)

CASEY COX

ISBN: 978-0-6489983-7-2

This book is a work of fiction. It really is. It has to be, otherwise the world really has gone mad. Any references to real people, organizations, media sites, types of alcohol, actors and locations are completely fictitious. Characters, names, plot points and dialogue are figments of the author's imagination.

SYNOPSIS

Scandal: (noun)
a: an action or event that causes a public feeling of shock and strong moral disapproval.
b: damage to reputation; public disgrace.
See also: Porter "I won't apologize for who I am" Jones.

A boy searching for the truth.
A Daddy with a lot to hide.

Porter Jones has always lived two lives. To the world, he's the mayor's smart, successful and savvy chief of staff. Conservative, yet charming. Good at his job, without overshadowing his boss.

But underneath the controlled persona, Porter's had to hide who he really is. A highly charged Dom with an unapologetically voracious appetite for sex, and that's putting it mildly.

But when a mayoral sex scandal thrusts him into the spotlight, Porter's private and public worlds collide. And the ruthless reporter who exposed the mayor now has his sights firmly on exposing Porter.

Declan Davies is doing life all wrong.

He's too nice to be the ruthless reporter he needs to be to get ahead. So when he digs into the mayor's past, he expects to maybe find a few unpaid parking tickets, not uncover Daylesford's biggest political scandal. He can't even do that right.

When Porter storms into Declan's office demanding answers, sparks fly. But if Porter thinks Declan will be a pushover, he's got another thing coming. And if Declan is obsessed with finding the truth, what will he do when he discovers who the real Porter Jones is?

SCANDAL
Scandal is a Daddy-lite enemies-to-lovers gay romance featuring a Dom Daddy with a lot to hide, and a curious boy obsessed with finding the truth.

Come along for the ride and enjoy some crazy/sexy/cool shenanigans, including: lots of off-the-record chats, bed bondage, spoon theory, sassy friends, lots of LOLs, and all the feels on the way to a heartwarming HEA.

Scandal is the fourth book in the *99 Daddies* series. Each book in the series will contain overlapping characters and storylines, so you may enjoy them more by reading them in order.

99 DADDIES
99 Daddies is a hilarious, entertaining, and heartwarming contemporary/new adult Daddy-lite MM romance series.

Escape to Daylesford, the (fictional) Daddy capital of America. If you love steamy and complex Daddy/boy dynamics, May-December gay romances with a twist, sweet and sassy MM age-gap romances, and chasing those guaranteed HEAs, you'll love it here.

So come along and meet the 99 Daddies of Daylesford. Who will be *YOUR* favorite?

CHAPTER ONE

PORTER

"Why the hell is my dick on the cover of *The Daylesford Times*, Porter?"

The mayor's angry voice drowned out the healing sounds of Tibetan bowls and the calm female voice that had been telling me the mantra of the day was to "see the positive side of every situation."

I opened my eyes to see Mayor William Smith storming into my office with a handful of newspapers in his arms, his expression furious and his nostrils flared. We really needed to do something about those nostrils, they were getting seriously out of hand.

I tapped pause on my guided meditation app as he strode over and proceeded to throw all of the newspapers he was carrying onto my desk. They landed with a disruptive—very un-Tibetan-bowl-like—thud.

I uncrossed my legs and leaned forward as William began to spread the newspapers out across my desk, giving me an unobstructed view of the day's headline in the city's most prestigious newspaper, *The Daylesford Times*.

Scandal! Mayor Willy's Willy Exposed

"William, what am I looking at here?"

I looked up at the man. The fury and nostril flaring had given way to a look of sheer terror.

Was this real?

Could it be?

I'd been Mayor Smith's chief of staff for nearly ten years. I knew him better than almost anyone else. He was just a few years older than me, but due to him being straight and the major Phil Collins vibe he gave off—with his capacious yet friendly face, bespectacled eyes and just-starting-to-recede hairline—I looked a good decade younger than him. At least.

But his wholesome, inoffensive, middle-aged "throwback to the '80s era in music" schtick was popular with voters for some strange, and annoying, reason. He was hands-down Daylesford's most popular mayor, always miles ahead of the opposition in the polls, even if most of his brilliant ideas came from me.

Most people thought that the chief of staff was essentially a glorified assistant, but it's so much more than that. I did all the grunt work and heavy lifting; he was just the face that went out there and sold it to the public. It wasn't exactly fair, and it was a situation that I had been hoping to change for some time.

I mean, I knew I could do the top job myself. I practically *was* doing it already. Plus, I knew I had looks, charisma, and people skills that left Mayor Smith in the dust.

But I'd never had an opening to make a move. It's kind of hard to replace someone so popular without it looking like a coup or some massive act of betrayal. That was not how I wanted to get to the top job.

I looked down again at the headlines and the accompanying blurry, pixelated selfie images sprawled across my desk.

"It's a semi-decent use of alliteration, and at least they used a lot of pixels," I said with a meek smile, trying to find the positive side of the situation.

I was met with a scowl, but continued unperturbed. "Lots of pixels means it looks like you have a large—"

"Porter." I knew that voice. That was the *I'm serious so don't fuck around with me* voice.

I pressed my fingers against my temples, trying to keep my last remaining zen intact, but it was too late. It was gone, and now I had this smoking heap of shit dumped on my desk to contend with.

"Alright, we need to get down to business. We need to talk, William," I said in a tone that reflected the seriousness of the situation. "If you could just close the..."

The mayor was just about to sit down and shot me a look.

I quickly got up and walked over to the door, closing it myself. I had to keep reminding myself of my place. Number two doesn't ask number one to close the door, he does it himself.

I returned to my desk, interlaced my fingers together, and looked Mayor William Smith straight in the eye.

"William, we are going to have a conversation, and I am going to need you to be completely honest with me."

He gave a quick nod, looking like he wanted to get this over and done with as quickly as possible.

He wasn't the only one.

"The first thing I need to know is..." I looked down again at the grainy images splashed on the front page of *The Daylesford Times* "...is this really you?"

He took off his thin-rimmed glasses and pinched the bridge of his nose with two fingers.

"It is." His voice was flat, dejected and filled with shame.

A shame I recognized all too well myself.

As someone who had what could be called a healthy sex drive, I was used to being judged by others. In that moment, I genuinely felt for the man.

I mean, I wasn't just a Daddy. I was also a Dom. A Dom that

liked to experiment and explore every facet of the kink lifestyle. From age play to role play, bondage to discipline, and everything in between, I had pretty much seen and done it all. Most of it several times over.

Although, unlike the mayor, I had the good sense to keep my sex life private. Well, maybe I shared a few of the finer details of my sexual adventures with my three closest friends, but that was it. The rest of my sexual proclivities stayed firmly shut in the vault, far from prying eyes and judging minds.

I only ever showed the outside world what I wanted people to see. A smart and successful chief of staff. If anything, I liked to give the impression that I was slightly conservative, careful to watch my language and even what I wore when I was in public. I could save the leather assless chaps for Revolver. In public I was all chinos and Ralph Lauren polos.

I was always friendly to the media and happy to press the flesh with the public, but I made sure to keep things in check and never commit the cardinal sin of overshadowing the main man himself.

At least, not until the right time came for me to make my move.

"So you got hacked?" I asked, trying to figure out how the man's cock had ended up as the day's headline.

The mayor winced. "Peggy and I started taking some photos like these"—he flailed his fingers around above the newspapers—"a few years ago. It was something that injected a little fun into our lives."

"Okay, that's good," I said, relieved.

"It is?" Every single wrinkle on the man's forehead was clearly visible as he looked at me.

"It is. It means this is a private act between a man and his wife. You weren't caught cheating by sending these images to another person, and your privacy was violated. Those two things work in our favor."

"Yeah, I guess they do." He didn't sound convinced, but I assumed his mind was racing. Not only was this deeply embarrassing for him, but I couldn't even imagine what his wife was going through.

"Where did you keep these photos?" I asked.

His phone hadn't been physically stolen, so it must have been a cyber hack.

"Peg and I have a Fallbox account," he admitted, somewhat sheepishly.

"Fallbox, really? Every celebrity sex scandal from the last five years has been linked to Fallbox. Why would you use them?"

"I don't know," William responded with an embarrassed shrug. "It's easy to use, I guess. And well, we use it to share photos—*other* kinds of photos—with family, so, we're familiar with it. You know me, Porter. I'm terrible with technology. I can barely write an email."

It was true. The man was a total tech luddite.

I took a deep, semi-calming breath as I looked him over. How could the man only be a few years older than me, yet still sound—and look—like a total Boomer?

"At least tell me you had it password protected, William."

He looked down at the floor before looking up at me. "Well, yeah, but..."

"But what?" I narrowed my eyes at him.

"It wasn't a very good password. It was zero, zero, zero...one."

"Oh for fuck's sake."

I slammed my hand on the desk so loudly that it startled him. With a password like that, he was practically inviting people to hack him.

"Here's what we'll do..." I began talking as I tried to bury thoughts about the truckload of work this scandal created for me.

"I'll reach out to Warren and ask him to prepare a response we can give to the press this morning." Warren was the best media spokesperson in the city, so I was sure he would be able to come up with something solid.

The mayor nodded appreciatively.

I continued. "And I'll speak to Kelly. Her team will work on the legal angle. Whoever did this needs to be caught and brought to justice."

For the first time that morning, the man's face softened with the slightest sign of relief.

"Thank you, Porter." His words were direct, but with a genuine warmth underneath.

I wasn't done with him yet.

"You know what they say, William. Where there is smoke, there's fire."

"What's that supposed to mean?" His jaw clenched as his beady, Phil Collins-esque eyes drilled into me.

It was my turn to use the *I'm serious so don't fuck around with me* voice. "Is there anything else I need to know? I mean *this* situation, I can manage. It's not great, obviously, but it's not the end of the world either. A husband sending his wife a dick pic won't end his career, but...is there anything else that might pop up that I need to be prepared for?"

He was meant to say no, maybe even laugh it off as a silly question to even ask him. After all, I knew the man's life story almost better than my own. You didn't ascend to any significant political position without having your entire background thoroughly vetted.

And the man's relationship history was pretty simple and straightforward. He'd only had two significant relationships. A high school sweetheart that lasted into the first year at college. Single for a year after that, but thankfully before social media, so no pics of frat parties or pranks that we had to worry about coming back to haunt him.

And then he met his current wife, Peggy, and they'd been together ever since. No kids, due to an unfortunate medical complication on her side, but otherwise, a perfectly happy and typical married couple.

The only even slightly salacious detail in the mayor's past was a one-night stand he had in between the two relationships. The interesting part was that it was with a man, his dorm roommate's older brother.

No one knew about it, though. The man had since gone on to a successful career in the business world. He was, by all accounts, happily married with three kids and probably just as keen to put the whole thing down to a drunken night of college debauchery-slash-experimentation as William was.

"Well, there is one other slight, little thing..."

William looked guilty, embarrassed, and pissed off, all at the same time.

I sat up a little taller in my seat, my fingers still interlaced and my shoulders drawn down my back. I was in brace position.

"Peggy and I like to do something that's a little...unusual, I guess you could say."

"Okay," I said with a friendly smile, trying to keep my face as neutral as possible. I had a sense he was going to open up and share something very private, and that vulnerability made me want to respond to him with nothing but open-hearted kindness.

"We're into...I mean, I enjoy it when...oh god, this is impossible."

He let out an exasperated sigh and stared up at the ceiling.

"Take your time, William," I said, reassuringly. "Whatever it is you're going to tell me, you know that I won't judge you for it, and of course, it goes without saying, it doesn't leave this office."

The mayor took one long breath in, and as he exhaled, he said, "I like getting pegged."

"Right." I knew I had to say something, and that was the best I could come up with on such short, unexpected notice.

"Pegging is..." he started to explain.

I raised my hand. "I know what pegging is, William."

"You do?" He sounded genuinely surprised.

Like I'd said, I had been very, *very* careful about the image I had crafted for myself, even with him.

Especially with him.

Politics was a dirty game, and I didn't want to give anyone any ammunition to be able to use against me. Even people who were on the same team and seemed friendly. I'd seen more than my fair share of people becoming traitors quicker than you could flip a dime.

No one apart from my three closest friends knew anything at all about my sex life, and that's exactly the way I intended for it to stay.

"The ass doesn't have a sexual orientation, William," I began. "Straight men can enjoy anal sex just as much as gay men. And here's one for you—not all gay men have anal sex."

"Really?"

"Yes, really."

I had learned a lot about that thanks to Hudson. I still felt a little bad about how I had reacted when he told me he was a side—that is, not clearly a top, bottom, or switch, and focused on communication and sexual pleasure other than penetration. It wasn't my proudest moment, because the last thing I ever wanted to do was to unintentionally sex-shame one of my best friends.

Thankfully, Hudson and I had made up before he and Liam headed off on their cross-country adventure. I still missed the guy heaps. The quad squad wasn't quite the same minus one.

"Oh, well, that's good to know, I guess," William said.

"Are there any photos...or videos...of you and Peggy...pegging?"

Holy shit. In a horror-filled instant, my mind flashed to the headlines this would create if the story ever broke.

Peggy Pegs the Mayor

How do you even begin to put a positive spin on *that*?

"No, never." William spoke definitively. "We're too, uh, busy, when we're doing it to be filming it."

That was a relief...I guess.

"Can I count on your help, Porter?"

I frowned.

What kind of a dumb-ass question was that?

My mind was already knee-deep in problem-solving mode, as always. Not only had I come up with every last significant policy of his for the last four or five years, I had been working diligently behind the scenes to improve his relationships with donors and Daylesford's powerful media and business elites.

"Of course, William." I bristled slightly, but tried to contain my displeasure and prevent it from pouring out of me. The man had enough to deal with at the moment. "You know I've got your back."

He cleared his throat. "Good. Look, I..."

I studied his face, I couldn't get a proper take on it.

"I know you have a bit of a reputation for being a..."

My tongue fell into the back of my throat. Surely not. He couldn't possibly have any idea of what I was into, could he? That I was a Daddy... A Dom...

"...a bit of a Samantha."

I smiled and grimaced at the same time.

I'd never been more grateful to hear that stupid nickname than I was right at that very moment. Another part of me was curious to know how he had found out about it, though. That was a nickname my closest friends had given me and only they knew about. Had he been eavesdropping on my private conversations?

That was a question I would definitely be coming back to later.

Even though that nickname was closely guarded, it wasn't the top-level secret other parts of me were. As long as that was all he knew, I could deal with that.

I looked down at my fingers. My grip had become so tight it had made my knuckles turn white. I guessed this was a topic that hit close to home. Maybe a little too close.

When a straight guy liked sex, he was simply a normal, red-blooded guy. If a woman or a gay man liked sex, they're...well, sluts. It's a totally bullshit double standard. I mean, it's the freakin' '20s after all—the 2020s, not the 1920s. But again, it served as a good reminder for me that I needed to keep my sex life hidden from public view at all costs.

"What are you saying, William?" I asked, trying to downplay the suspicion in my tone.

"I think that you're uniquely positioned to understand what I am going through, so...I want you to track down the reporter that broke the story, speak to him, and fix this mess up."

"You don't want Warren or anyone from the media team to..."

"No," he interrupted forcefully. "I want you on this and only you. Track down the reporter, find out if he knows anything else and who the fucking scumbag source of this is."

William stood up to leave. "This requires a level of discretion I am sure you are familiar with," he said, opening the door.

It was too early in the morning for the mayor's passive-aggressive bullshit. I forced a smile as he left, closing the door behind him with a loud bang, and reminded myself of the day's mantra: try to see the positive in every situation.

Well, at least on the positive side, tracking down this reporter shouldn't be too hard. I grabbed the copy of the newspaper and looked at the byline.

Declan Davies.

Well, Declan, I thought to myself, *you and I are going to have a little chat.*

Three days later...

I slammed the receiver down and let out a loud, "Fucking hell."

I dragged my fingers over my face.

Damn, this wasn't as easy as I thought it was going to be. Declan Davies was proving to be one hard-to-pin-down asshole reporter.

Despite repeated attempts to try and reach the guy, I'd only ever gotten as far as *The Daylesford Times'* front desk. All twenty-seven emails I had sent him had resulted in exactly zero replies back.

So I did a little digging on the guy.

He was new to the paper. A kid, basically. A junior reporter only a few years out of college who, from what I could tell, normally did fluffy human interest stories such as giving an exclusive insight into the winners of Daylesford's annual flower show or covering Mrs. Langley's one hundredth birthday, with a bonus inside scoop featuring her top tips for how to live a long, healthy life.

How he'd veered into the political lane and broken the most controversial political story since Councilor Nguyen waded into the political no-go zone of commenting on the winner of *The Bachelor* was just one of the many questions I had for him.

But first, I needed the guy to get back to me. And I needed that to happen soon, before the mayor got even more pissed off at me that it had already taken this long.

And right on cue...

The mayor burst into my office, stared me down like he was a cowboy in a Western, cocked his head, and demanded, "Well?"

I winced. "Sorry, I still can't get through, William. I've been trying nonstop for the last three days. He's just brushing me off big time, for some reason."

"Then what the fuck are you still doing here, Porter? If he's not getting back to you, then you need to go to him."

I sighed, knowing he was right.

I had avoided going to the reporter because hey, nothing looked more like being the mayor's lackey than, well, being the mayor's lackey.

But it had to be done.

I grabbed my car keys and headed over to the headquarters of *The Daylesford Times*.

CHAPTER TWO

DECLAN

"Another round!" Shannon cried out as the guys let out a boozy round of cheers in agreement.

"I'll get it," I said loudly enough for them all to hear me, as I shuffled my way out of the corner booth. After all, we were all here celebrating the massive story I had just broken.

To say that these guys were big hitters would have been a massive understatement. In the almost twelve months I had worked at *The Daylesford Times*, none of the guys sitting in the booth around me had given me so much as a second glance.

Shannon McCormack, Lane Marshall, Neil Brown, and Alex Palmer were the who's who of investigative reporters. They were *The Daylesford Times'* best and brightest, which meant they were amongst some of the best reporters in the entire country. The paper was one of the most prestigious and influential in the US, often setting not just the local and state agendas, but the national one as well.

Normally, these guys were the ones breaking hard-hitting, political stories like a mayoral sex scandal. And yet, here they all were...for me.

Celebrating me.

The least I could do was buy them a round of drinks. *Another* round of drinks.

I silently thanked myself that I had been saving as hard as I had been in recent months. I'd never been to the bar that we were at before, but each round was costing me almost as much as I spent on groceries for the entire week.

"Same again?" I asked as I got to my feet. I felt a slight headrush. I must have stood up too quickly. I was sure it had nothing to do with the three—or wait, maybe it was four—margaritas I had consumed. But hey, I was just keeping up, although looking around at them, these guys didn't look as unsteady as I felt. I guess being in the big league built up your tolerance to alcohol.

"Sure, kid," one of them, I wasn't sure who, said as I picked up on the slightest hint of a dismissive air in his voice. A faint laugh muffled into the background as I walked over to the bar and ordered the next round of drinks.

I spied a jug of water with some glasses next to it at the far end of the bar as I waited for the bartender to serve me. I made my way over and poured myself a glass. I didn't have much experience with business lunches like this, but so far there was a whole lot of boozing and not a whole lot of eating.

If I wanted to make it to the entrees, I had to slow down a little bit. I drank a whole glass, before pouring myself another one and downing it too.

There, that was a little better.

I placed my order with the bartender, who said he would get someone to bring it over to us, and made my way back to the table. I stopped for a moment before rejoining them.

I still couldn't believe it. I was having lunch with the four men who were essentially my biggest heroes. I mean, I couldn't exactly blame them for ignoring me when I was nothing more than a newbie nobody. They were important, distinguished and very accomplished reporters. My experience to date (other than my year at *The Daylesford Times*) was co-editor at the Daylesford University magazine and two years as a junior reporter at *The Daylesford Tribune*. Hardly anything to write home about.

Now I was a junior reporter at *The Daylesford Times,* which meant I had absolutely no reason to even be on their radar at all. Most of my pieces were so fluffy and frivolous, I doubted they had even read them. For some reason, I just never got the chance to work on anything more exciting than a county fair or a flower show.

In this line of work, you had to be ruthless in order to get ahead. That was one of the things I struggled with most. I wanted to cover meaningful stories, but I didn't understand why I had to be a total jerk to do that.

But as I was quickly learning, nice guys really did finish last...or reporting on why this year's roses weren't as big as last year's, as the case may be.

Until now, that is.

I had become a reporter because I believed in the truth. It really was as simple as that. My curiosity about life started as a kid and with what I thought was a relatively simple question I had asked my mom when I was in second grade. "Why do the other kids at school have a dad and I don't?"

Even at that young age, I could tell that the answer she gave me, while well-intentioned, was far from the truth. Years later, when she sat me down and told me that my father had left her the day he found out she was pregnant with me, I knew that even that wasn't quite the full story, either.

The only thing I never doubted growing up was how much my mother loved me. She worked three jobs to support us, yet I never felt like she was missing from my life.

Somehow, she was always there for me when I needed her, being the best mom in the world. Though we lacked when it came to practical means and creature comforts, we overflowed with love, affection and stability. That's really all a kid needed, and for giving me that, I would do anything for her.

It wasn't until my final year at Daylesford University that I put my journalism degree to its first, practical, real-world application. I finally managed to pry the entire story out of my mom, including the name of my biological father.

I adjusted my shoulders in my slightly too-large suit as I sat back down at the booth. "Drinks are on their way," I said happily, but no one really seemed to notice me.

These guys were hard to read.

When they talked to you, they made you feel like you were the only person in the world that they were interested in. I guess that's part of what made them such good reporters. They made people feel safe and were able to establish a high degree of trust very quickly.

But when they ignored you, it felt like the *worst* thing.

I just wanted them to accept me. I knew I wouldn't become their peer overnight. I wasn't expecting that. I had years—no, decades—of hard work ahead of me to reach that status. But surely they could let me in a little bit, say hello once in a while, acknowledge my existence in the elevator? Was that too much to ask?

Maybe it was.

"So Declan," Lane said with a hearty slap on my shoulder. A searing pain shot through my body at the touch, but I did my best to mask it. He was *The Daylesfords Times'* senior political reporter and the man I respected the most out of the group. "Tell us, how exactly did you get the scoop on the mayor?"

"Yeah, Declan," Neil chimed in. He was the senior finance and business reporter, but his narrow eyes and oily skin always gave me an icky feeling about him. "Who's your source?"

The waitress came over with our drinks, handing everyone another ginormous margarita. I raised my glass in the air, thinking a toast might have been in order, but no one followed suit, so I quickly brought the salt-rimmed glass to my lips and took a sip.

"A reporter never reveals their sources," I said, trying to balance sounding smug with what I thought a big-time reporter would say. I mean, that was what they would say, wasn't it? Heck, I really had no clue and was starting to wish I could reduce myself down to the size of a Lego toy and drown myself in my margarita.

"Good answer," Lane said, unconvincingly. The men's eyes darted around at each other, as if they were communicating in a silent, foreign language.

I mean, they weren't exactly going to divulge their sources to me. Why should I tell them who my source was? I might have been young and eager for their approval, but I wasn't that naive.

The men returned to whatever it was they were talking about, which left me alone with my margarita and mulling over the events that had led me to breaking the salacious story. I wish I could have said it was due to my amazing investigative skills.

The truth was unfortunately a little less impressive than that. A chance, late-night online encounter in a political forum led to an unexpected chat with someone who put me in touch with someone who, in turn, put me in touch with someone else, who happened to be an expert dark web hacker.

Over the course of a few weeks, the more I chatted with the still anonymous and unknown-to-me hacker, the more I realized they were legit. Well, as legit as a cyber hacker could be.

So I asked them for a little...help.

I was just coming off the Mrs. Langley 100-year birthday story, and as sweet and inspiring as the lady truly was, I was on the lookout for something a little meatier for my next piece. The annual Daylesford flower show was coming up fast, and I didn't want to get stuck covering it...again.

So late one evening, I asked the hacker—who I only knew by their username of time2telldatruth—if they could do me a little favor.

It was simple, really. I just wanted to get some dirt on the mayor. I had exhausted all of the normal channels, even extensively going through every single published article about the man during his sixteen-year political career, from the time he started as a local councilor and spanning the entire decade of his mayorship.

The only thing I got for all of that time and effort was a big fat lot of nada. The man was clean. Publicly, anyway. But I knew he had secrets. Who didn't? Someone who was that clean had to be hiding a skeleton or two in their closet.

Luckily for me, time2telldatruth was up for the challenge. They'd been talking to me about the dark web, which, even though I pretended to understand, I still couldn't quite wrap my brain around. And from the bits and pieces that I had managed to grasp about it, I was perfectly happy to leave it that way. It didn't sound like a great place, so I settled on remaining blissfully ignorant of the internet's dark and twisted underbelly.

But time2telldatruth knew what they were doing and were more than happy to get their hands dirty on my behalf. In all honesty, I was hoping maybe they'd uncover some unpaid parking tickets or maybe that the mayor was a bad tipper or a tyrant to work for.

Even though I had every reason to, I didn't want to discover anything too...personal.

But then time2telldatruth found the images—those intimate, naked images—well, I knew what I had to do. I didn't have any other option, really.

I had to report on them and tell the truth.

The reaction to my story in the seventy-two hours since it had come out had set off a tidal wave of furor that I had never experienced before. The story went viral instantly, and that night, I was watching late night shows and seeing my story covered by all the major programs. I didn't think it was possible to make Ben & Jerry's taste any better. Turns out, there was.

The editor of *The Daylesford Times* stopped by my work

cubicle to congratulate me herself that morning. She had been barely gone a minute when these four guys came up to me and offered to take me out for lunch later in the week to celebrate.

Everyone wanted a piece of me.

In some ways, it felt good to get recognition from the editor and from senior reporters I admired so much. But I also knew that it was fleeting. If I didn't capitalize on the momentum I had created and follow this up with another big story, I'd be back at that flower show covering the secret ingredient Mrs. Anderson added to her potting mix for extra large roses.

"Is Jones hounding you?" Alex's question caught me off guard.

"Who?" I replied.

"Porter Jones, the mayor's chief of staff," Alex said in a voice that suggested I should have immediately known who he was talking about.

"Oh yeah, constantly," I said, taking another sip of my drink. "Phone calls, emails. The works. I—I never reply to him, of course."

"Good, keep that little bitch at bay for as long as you can, Declan," Alex said.

It wasn't just the vulgarity of his words, although they were bad enough, but there was something in the way he said it that sent a cold shiver through me.

The other men began chuckling amongst themselves.

"That guy is such a total slut." Lane leaned over to fill me in. "Rumor has it that he's slept with pretty much every single guy under the age of twenty-five in Daylesford."

"Oh."

I frowned and looked at the men, all seasoned reporters who were used to covering the most important stories of the day, acting like bitchy, gossipy school kids.

It didn't sit right with me, and I shuddered. Was this what being a ruthless reporter looked and sounded like?

I had been ignoring Porter Jones because he had a reputation for being charming, ruthless, and always getting what he wanted. Professionally, that was. I had never heard anyone at the office mention anything about his private life at all.

I was worried that if I spoke to him, he'd have a way of finding out who my source was. Or that he would manipulate me in some way with his intriguing smile. I might have seen a few clips of the man while I had been doing my research into the mayor, and I couldn't deny the truth, the man was drop-dead gorgeous.

He was well built, with short ashy blond hair and slightly too-large ears, but it was his smile and uneven eyes that I found to be the most interesting features about him. I first noticed it in a few photos, but it was video form that really did it justice.

When he smiled, like *really* smiled, a funny thing happened. His left eye got smaller, but his right eye got bigger. It sounded like it should have looked weird or creepy, but it was nothing short of heartwarmingly delectable.

I tuned out as the men returned to another topic. But maybe this was what it took? If I wanted to make it as a serious reporter, I had to continue keeping Porter Jones at a distance. I was sure it's what all of the men sitting around me would have done. So if I wanted to be like them and get taken seriously as a reporter that could cover more than human interest stories, I guess it was what I had to do.

I looked down at my cell phone and checked the time. "Oh man. You guys, it's ten past two."

Somehow, we'd been here for more than three hours and still hadn't had any food.

"So? Relax." Neil waved his hand dismissively at me, before grabbing a napkin and wiping it over his greasy forehead.

"I have to go," I said, making it to my feet. I had a shit-ton to work on. None of the other guys made a move or even looked in my direction.

I stood up and adjusted my shoulders, flinching at the pain that thundered in my lower back. I took a deep breath, trying to get at least a little more comfortable. Constant pain that throbbed in the background, I had gotten used to. It was the sudden, sharp bursts that terrorized me.

"Are you guys coming or what?"

"We'll catch up with you, Declan," Lane said, not even bothering to turn his head to look at me.

"Suit yourselves." I took the last swig of my margarita and headed back to the office.

Ten minutes and one slightly margarita-induced, dizzying Uber ride later, I walked in through the front doors of *The Daylesford Times* office. I still smiled every time I made my way through the impressive ground floor lobby.

I worked here. Even after a year, it still hadn't fully sunk in. Here I was, making my way up the ladder at this incredible, iconic institution.

I jumped into the elevator, and a few short moments later, the doors opened, and I stepped out onto the fifth floor.

"Hey, Mon," I said to the receptionist, flashing my widest smile and speaking with all the confidence of a big-time reporter in-the-making. "Love that dress," I added with a jazzy snap of the fingers. Okay, the jazzy finger snap was definitely traceable to the margaritas making their way through my system.

"Uh, Declan." She raised her hand in the air, her face looking bemused. "Porter Jones has been trying to reach you. Again."

I let out a laugh. A loud and confident one, like what Lane or any of the other guys would have done. "So what's new?"

"What's new," a male voice suddenly filled the air, "is that I am standing right here, Mr. Davies."

I gulped and slowly pivoted towards the voice. My gaze was met by two limpid eyes and a set of firmly pursed lips.

"Porter Jones," the man said, extending his hand out as he stepped in toward me, never once looking away.

I steadied myself, wiping my palm along the back of my trousers discreetly. I smiled, staring back at him as intently as my buzzed-blurry eyes would allow.

"Declan Davies." Our fingers met and a torrent of warmth filled my chest, almost knocking me off my feet. It was the margaritas. It had to be. That fifth one might have been a little too much for a Thursday afternoon.

"Nice—nice to meet you," I stammered.

"Yes," Porter agreed, giving my hand a firm squeeze. "It's good to meet you too, Declan...finally."

CHAPTER THREE

PORTER

"Right this way," Declan managed to say in a relatively normal voice as I followed him away from the reception area and down a long, narrow corridor. "We can talk in my office," he said as he held the door open to what was clearly a boardroom.

As I stepped past him and into the brightly lit room, I caught the distinct whiff of alcohol on his breath. I gave him a knowing head nod, but didn't say anything. He closed the door, and I turned to him. He still had a *deer-caught-in-headlights* look about him, but it had reduced slightly during the short walk from the reception area to his office-slash-boardroom.

"Please, sit down," he said, pointing to the impressive oak wood table that could comfortably seat at least twenty people. I made my way over to the far side of the room and began to walk alongside the table, running my fingers over the backs of the chairs.

Declan followed me from the other side of the table, his eyes carefully observing my every movement. He was holding on to the backs of the chairs as well, but I got the distinct impression that it was more for support and to hold himself upright than anything else.

My first impression of the man was that he had the face of a supermodel—with gorgeous wavy brown hair that fell forward over his forehead, long eyebrows over two wide hazel eyes, a full lower lip, and a slight groove in his chin—and the legs of Bambi. Given it was half past two and he was only just stumbling back from what I imagined was a long lunch celebrating his exclusive scoop, that part didn't surprise me.

What did surprise me was the completely ill-fitting and totally unflattering suit he was wearing. Or swimming in, to be more accurate. It was a look that even a used car salesman would have distanced himself from. I couldn't even begin to describe what color it was because it was so ugly I was pretty certain that the particular hue had been banned sometime during the mid '90s. But if I had to describe it, I'd go with the kind of blue you'd imagine dolphin spit to look like.

I reached the head of the table and sat down. Declan chose the seat right next to me, and our knees touched briefly as he sat down as well.

"Sorry," he breathed heavily, apologizing for the accidental knee knock.

It was at that moment that I noticed his hands were shaking. I looked deep into his hazel eyes. They were dark and...hiding something. I looked back down at his hands, but he had placed them in his lap, holding them down so they wouldn't continue betraying him.

"We have an issue," I began sharply. "Your story about Mayor Smith."

"What about it?" he snapped at me, but the look on his face suggested that his aggressive tone had surprised him more than me.

"What about it?" I repeated, slightly incredulous. "How about the fact that you have invaded the mayor's, and his wife's, privacy, not only severely embarrassing them both personally, but also inflicting a whole ton of political damage too, Declan?"

His shoulders slumped down, and he looked forlorn for a moment, before he sat up and straightened himself up again.

"I'm a reporter, Mr.—Porter," he quickly corrected himself. I'd used his first name on purpose. It was a common tactic to establish dominance. "It's my job to report the facts."

He tilted his head to the side, which I took as a sign that he was silently daring me to respond.

"These aren't just facts, Declan," I replied matter-of-factly. "This is a gross invasion of two people's privacy."

He opened and closed his mouth a few times, unable to settle on a response.

So I continued instead. "We're talking about two consenting adults engaging in a private sexual activity. This doesn't relate to any aspect of the mayor's performance in his work capacity, nor is it a matter that has any impact or consequence for the constituents of Daylesford. So Declan, can you please explain to me why you ran this story?"

I started tapping my fingers loudly on the table. Another little strategic mind tactic, again to establish my authority over him.

He stared at me silently and ran his tongue over his lips. "I don't have to explain anything to you, Porter"—he tugged at his too-long shirt sleeve—"I was just doing my job."

"Oh, I'm sorry, I thought you were a reporter," I said sarcastically. "I remember a time when reporters had a sense of decency and integrity." I scoffed before going on. I was kind of on a roll. "And they weren't just vultures interested in exposing the most salacious, intimate details of people's lives for no good reason."

"I have a good reason," Declan fought back, and I had to say, despite looking a little weary and unsteady on his feet at first, underneath it all, the guy had nerves of steel. I liked that. "The public has a right to know."

"Is that so?" I asked, folding my arms across my chest and

throwing an unimpressed look in his direction. "Does the public also have a right to know everything about, hmmm, let's say you, Declan Davies?"

His eyes widened before he looked around the room, deliberately avoiding me. It seemed that my question had touched a rawer nerve than I had been expecting. For the briefest of moments, I wondered why.

I looked at him sitting across from me in his ill-fitting suit and in what appeared to be a post-boozy-lunch stupor. What could a guy like him know about being exposed and humiliated for what he was into sexually? Or for who he was?

He couldn't, because the most traumatic experience of his life to date would have probably been suit shopping.

Unlike me.

I knew a thing—or twenty—about traumatic experiences because of your sexuality.

My parents disowned me the second they discovered that I was gay. It was in my final year of high school when I came back home from school one day to find both of my parents sitting at the formal dining table. As I approached them, my heart stopped in my chest as I saw all of my magazines neatly piled in front of them.

My secret stash of gay pornographic magazines.

Given how strict and controlling they were, I hadn't wanted to risk anything by going on the internet to explore my sexuality. So I turned to old-fashioned magazines to get my fix. They weren't exactly a reliable source of information, but they did confirm one thing for sure: I was attracted to men.

The magazines were my only escape, the only outlet I had for my sexuality. I had no one in my family to talk to about it, I was too scared to speak to any of my friends at school, and I was too young to be able to go out to clubs or bars to meet people.

Under the dining table, my parents had conveniently packed a bag with all of my clothes in it. I can still remember the look in my mother's eyes as she handed the bag to my dad, the disgust and shame so clearly written across her face. My father dropped the bag into my hands, as if he didn't even want to touch me.

I came *this close* to ending up on the streets, but somehow managed to get through my last year of high school by staying at friends' homes and changing locations every few weeks, before I could wear my welcome out. It was horrible and stressful and lonely, but I was determined not to let it affect my grades.

I got a full scholarship to Daylesford University and fell in love with the city from the moment I arrived to start my new life. In short succession, I met three guys who would become my new family. Stirling, Steel, and Hudson weren't just friends—they were my brothers.

For the last twenty years, they were by my side through it all. The good, the bad, and the ugly. They loved, supported, and encouraged me in ways my so-called real family never had.

College wasn't all just getting drunk at frat parties and being late to lectures. For me, it was a turning point in my life. It was the first time I could be free to explore who I really was, without any shame or guilt or need to hide.

So I took to it with all of the abandon of a person who had been suppressed for his entire life. When your family thought you were an abomination and literally kicked you out of the home you grew up in, you had two choices. You could believe them and go down a path of self-hatred that was almost impossible to overcome, or you could give them the biggest middle finger of your life and live your life however you chose.

I went for option B.

That's why I leaned into my sexuality in the way that I had. I made a vow to myself that I would never feel bad, ashamed, or apologetic for having a high and healthy sex drive. And I refused to be sorry for being into kink and being a part of the lifestyle.

A lot of people had misconceptions about the kink community. They thought it was all a group of sexual deviants and perverts who only got their thrills by flogging, spanking, or inflicting all sorts of pain on each other.

That couldn't have been any further from the truth. The kinksters I had encountered in Daylesford were some of the most loving, caring, and compassionate people I had ever met. They came from all walks of life. Doctors and lawyers, teachers, nurses, and cleaners. Young and old. Wild to mild. It really was the full spectrum of the kink rainbow.

Sure, their sexual proclivities weren't to everyone's tastes, but they would never judge anyone for what they were into or, I don't know, kick a seventeen-year-old out onto the streets with no money and not so much as a handshake.

The biggest irony of my life so far was that I had chosen a profession that had, in fact, pushed me back into the closet. At least as far as kink went.

The people of Daylesford were generally pretty progressive, and my sexuality wasn't even an issue politically. In fact, I think that if anyone ever tried to use it as a weapon against me, it would backfire against them.

But kink?

The sad truth was that we still lived in a world that had a lot of bigoted misconceptions about the kink lifestyle. I knew that right from the get-go, which was why I had compartmentalized my life as fastidiously as I had.

My work life and my sex life were completely closed off to one another, never intertwining or connected to each other in even the slightest of ways. My only true outlet, the only time I could really open myself up in front of others, was with Stirling, Steel, and Hudson. Only they knew the true me. I trusted them with all of the juicy details I knew they secretly liked hearing about, even if they loved to joke that they didn't.

My career choice and, up until this point, my clandestine political ambitions also meant that I'd never had the time nor inclination to pursue a serious relationship. Frankly, I didn't really see the need to.

I got my kicks whenever I needed them, either through any of the many apps I used or at my almost-weekly visits to Revolver. Men were like a tap I could turn on, or off, at any given moment. Why would I want to complicate things by having feelings and emotions and, dear lord, a relationship?

At least that's what I tried to convince myself.

The truth was that despite having tried everything—every sex act imaginable, every sexual position known to humankind—I hadn't been able to find any one thing that really...stuck.

Maybe that was my problem. I wasn't able to actually find anything to really and truly fulfill me. I'd gone too hard and done too much, and now I was destined to a lifetime of easy, casual, no-strings sex.

Fun in the moment, but a life spent...alone.

"I need some water," Declan said, standing up. He walked over, steadying himself against the wall, to a wood-paneled mini-fridge at the other end of the table. He opened it and grabbed himself a bottle of water.

"Want one?" he asked, looking over his shoulder at me.

I shook my head. "You don't have anything stronger...in your office?"

A rosy blush filled his cheeks as he returned to his seat.

I ran my eyes up and down his body, wondering what lay underneath that grossly-too-large suit he was wearing. Was he smooth and lithe? Was he a little hairy and packing some nice, tight muscles? Did he like getting tied up and surrendering to his master?

Wait, where the hell did that come from?

My mouth felt dry, and I suddenly wished I hadn't turned down his offer of water.

"I really don't know what you want from me," he said after

taking a drink from the bottle. His lips were still slightly wet, glistening almost teasingly under the bright boardroom lights.

But I wasn't thinking about the words he had just said. I was imagining what his red lips would look like wrapped around my cock. Whether he would submit easily or whether he would make me work for it.

I liked working for it.

"What I want from you, Declan," I said, moving in closer and delicately running my fingers over his forearm, "is for you to stop writing articles about the mayor's sex life."

Declan's eyes followed my hands as I placed them onto the table beside his arm and resumed tapping away loudly.

He reached shakily for his water bottle and gulped down the rest of it thirstily.

I continued moving in even closer to Declan, so that our faces were mere inches apart. His skin looked so soft, and I had the sudden urge to run my fingers across his cheekbone and down under the ridge of his square jawline.

He was breathing heavily, but the smell of alcohol had almost left him. He was sobering up and didn't quite know how to sit, where to look, or what to do with himself.

I pulled away and sank into the back of my chair.

He needed space, and I needed to study his face.

Declan Davies wasn't what I had been expecting. I had assumed I was dealing with a ruthless reporter, one who had an inability—and lacked the basic decency—to return a phone call or email.

But that wasn't who Declan was.

Or, at least, not entirely.

It took someone who'd been putting on an act his whole life to recognize when someone else was doing the same. And that's exactly what Declan was doing—showing the world something he thought they wanted to see.

But it wasn't who he actually was.

I saw the tells. I knew them well enough myself.

The way he would cock his head to the side after he'd said something, as if he was mentally checking in with himself to make sure he hadn't misspoken. Or the way he tugged nervously at his shirt sleeve, trying to give off an air of confidence but only really exposing his own self-consciousness.

And that ridiculous fucking suit.

Unless I had missed the latest hipster fad of ironic fashion, that suit was a cry for...something.

As I looked at his face, his heavy breathing, his completely on-edge disposition, I didn't see a ruthless reporter. All I saw was a young man who was hiding something.

And whatever that something was, I was overcome with a sudden, profound, and completely inexplicable urge to uncover exactly what it could be.

CHAPTER FOUR

DECLAN

Note to self: no more day drinking. It only leads to bad things.

Like not being able to walk straight.

Or think clearly.

Or resist succumbing to the charmingly ruthless Porter Jones.

He was even more attractive in real life than in all of the photos and videos I had seen of him.

My initial instinct to avoid him had proven to be right, but it was kind of hard to ignore the man when he was sitting in the waiting lounge...waiting for me.

I did my best to appear cool, calm, and collected, like the big-time reporter I was on my way to becoming, but I wasn't sure how well I had managed to pull it off. Something as simple as walking in a straight line was proving to be a harder feat to pull off than normal.

Then my brain stupidly tried to convince me that Porter would believe the boardroom was actually my office. Worse yet, my mouth agreed with my brain and shot off before I could do anything about it, like shutting the fuck up and not making up an incredibly ridiculous lie.

All in all, I wasn't sure what kind of a first impression I made on Porter, but I definitely wasn't putting my best foot forward.

He, on the other hand, was the epitome of professionalism and confidence. Just like my junior colleagues had told me he would be. And absolutely nothing like what my senior colleagues had dismissed him as.

He gave off nothing but clean-cut, wholesome vibes, perfectly wrapped up in a suit that looked like it was made to accentuate his broad shoulders and slim waist. Oh, wait, it probably was.

Only I was stupid enough to go to an outlet mall in search of my business attire. And only I was the kind of sucker who fell for the saleslady's sob story—her husband had left her for a younger woman, and her kids were giving her a hard time at home—and ended up feeling so bad for her that I bought every last remaining suit she had on sale.

In a way, buying suits that were at least two sizes too large for me was a good thing. It made it almost impossible for anyone who didn't know me to see my secret shame. Sure, I might have looked like some smarmy, small-town politician, but at least no one could tell I had a condition that I had been desperately hiding my whole life.

The sound of Porter's fingers tapping impatiently on the boardroom table stirred me back to life. He was looking at me expectantly, as if it was my turn to speak or something.

Shit. What the hell was I supposed to say?

This impromptu meeting had definitely sobered me up some, but I still wasn't at the point where I could do complicated things like operate heavy machinery or, you know, think clearly.

What would Lane do? Or Shannon, or Alex, or even oily-faced Neil, if they were in the exact same situation?

They wouldn't let themselves be intimidated, that's for damn sure.

Porter was trying every trick in the book, and given I was slightly incapacitated due to downing five margaritas at a food-free lunch, it was kind of working.

Well, it *had* been working.

If Porter Jones thought he could march into my office—well, boardroom—in his expensive, tailor-made suit and exude the kind of confidence that made people fall under his magical spell, then he had another thing coming.

"Porter, I'm a very busy man," I said as my fingers joined his on the boardroom table, and I began knocking away too. Two could play at this finger-tapping game.

His gaze was drawn to my fingers, and it looked like a small smirk stretched his lips for just the slightest moment. I began knocking harder, wanting my table-tapping to be louder than his.

His smirk, or whatever it was, faded as I continued. "And I'm sorry, but I don't have time for this."

I winced.

Don't apologize, dummy.

"I mean, I'm not sorry..."

Shit, don't highlight the accidental apology by drawing more attention to it.

Come on brain, I know you're in there. *Wake up!*

"I just...don't have time for this."

There, that was better. Why hadn't I just said that from the beginning?

I arched an eyebrow and gave him the best dismissive once-over I could. I was pleasantly surprised at how easy acting like an asshole reporter was turning out to be. Maybe I was starting to pull it off?

"Cat got your tongue, Porter?" I added for good measure as I started to swing in my seat.

Wait, swivelling was bad. Childish. I gripped the edge of the table to stop myself from rocking in my chair like a fifth grader.

I could see his jaw was firmly clenched. His light green eyes zeroed in on me. He had stopped tapping on the table. The only audible sound in the room was each breath passing in and out of his nose.

I had no idea what he was going to do next, but I had a sneaking suspicion that underneath his slick demeanor, he was boiling up, like a volcano about to explode. I gripped the table harder, preparing for what was to come.

"I'm very sorry to have taken up your time, Mr. Davies," he said, standing up.

Well...that was unexpected.

Why was he getting up? Was he leaving? I didn't want him to leave.

Wait, why didn't I want him to leave?

He began walking to the door. I scrambled to my feet and followed close behind him.

When he got to the door, he turned around to face me. He looked serious, almost stern, and in that moment, I felt a sadness sweep over me that I hadn't gotten to see his expression that had so charmed me in his videos.

The goofy look he made when he smiled and his eyes did that funny, uneven-bulgey thing that they did.

He blinked a few times, and his face softened into a less sour, more neutral expression.

"I enjoy a very good working relationship with most of Daylesford's media. And I look forward to developing an equally positive relationship with you, Mr. Davies."

Suddenly, I found myself wishing we were back on a first-name basis.

He stretched his hand out, and I looked down at his perfectly manicured fingers.

For some reason, I didn't want to shake his hand. I just wanted to pull those fingers in toward me and, I don't know, have them rough up my hair a little.

What the hell was that?

I held back a little choke that was bubbling up in the back of my throat as I stretched out my hand to meet his.

The sudden shift in his behavior was making me woozy...and not in a good way.

Was it a sign that my power play had worked? He did start calling me Mr. Davies, after all. That was a sign of respect that had been missing from our interaction right from the very start.

Maybe this was what it felt like to be cutthroat and hard, like a big league reporter? If it was, it certainly wasn't a feeling I was enjoying. It was cold, and alienating, and utterly unpleasant.

We shook hands, but the touch was clinical.

"I look forward to having a positive relationship with you, too...Mr. Jones."

"I'll let myself out. I know the way."

And with a half-hearted smile that didn't reach anywhere near his eyes, he left.

I turned back to face the empty, brightly lit boardroom, stuck on how alone I suddenly felt. I walked over to the chairs to tidy them up, grabbed my empty water bottle, switched the light off, and sullenly made my way back to my actual office. Or, more accurately, cubicle.

As I reached my desk, a pair of excited blue eyes peered up over the divider wall.

"Where have you been?" Mel, a fellow junior reporter and my cubicle neighbor, asked suspiciously.

"I've been in meetings," I replied, sitting down and grimacing as the first shot of pain sparked in my lower back.

"Sure, sure," she said, and even though I couldn't see her lips, I could tell she was smiling.

"Are you okay?" Her eyes zeroed in on me as a deep frown spread across her forehead.

"Just...the usual," I said lamely.

Mel was the only person I had told about my condition. She had started at the paper three months before I did, but from my very first day, she took me under her wing, and we'd been close ever since. She had a protective instinct and would always look out for me. I trusted her.

Before I knew it, she had turned the corner, grabbed a spare chair, and rolled up next to me. Her sweet, flowery perfume filled the air around us.

"Who were your meetings with?"

"What meetings?" I asked absently.

"Ah ha, busted!" Mel said with a laugh. She reached out her hand to touch me playfully but withdrew it, remembering how much it would hurt.

Damn.

"I was out at lunch," I said as I switched my computer on.

A coy smile stretched her brightly painted red lips. "For four hours?"

I knew she had an article due that day, so she was doing what she typically did when she had a looming deadline: procrastinating.

I sighed.

Mel wouldn't stop until she got what she wanted, so in other words, she was going to be a killer reporter in no time.

"Lane, Shannon, Alex, and Neil took me out for lunch."

"Ooh, the big-timers." Her eyes sparkled. "Impressive."

"Well, actually, come to think of it, I think I took them out."

She sent a puzzled look my way. "What do you mean?"

"Well, I paid for at least four out of the five rounds of drinks."

"Wait," she said, lifting her hand in the air, her fingernails covered in matching red nail polish. "Two questions. One, if they were taking you out to celebrate your awesome success, why weren't they paying for drinks? And two, if you were paying for drinks, please tell me you used the corporate credit card?"

Shit, the corporate credit card. I totally forgot.

Of course I should have been using that and not my own. That's why the guys were laughing every time I went to the bar to order another round. I wasn't sure what was happening at the time, but it was starting to make sense now.

I cringed at my own stupidity.

Who was I to think I could mix with them? I'd never fit in. I'd never be one of them, if for no other reason than I wasn't the kind of person who could laugh at other people's mistakes.

Professionally, those guys were my heroes, but personally, I was starting to see them for the assholes that they were.

"Of course I used the corporate credit card, Mel," I said, injecting my voice with a believable air of confidence––at least, I hoped that's how it sounded.

Judging by her face, Mel wasn't buying it.

She very gently, almost so softly that I couldn't feel it, placed her hand on my shoulder.

"Declan, you know I'm super stoked for your success, right?"

I nodded. "Of course I know you are."

The moment the article was released online, she called me, and spent two minutes screaming non-stop.

"And I think it's great that the big-timers are finally acknowledging your existence, but..."

She bit down on her red lip, and the frown returned to her face.

"Just say it, Mel," I said as I looked over at her.

"Those guys are jackasses."

Tell me about it.

"And you're not," she continued. "You will make it and be successful one day, Declan. And you can do it without turning into one of *them*."

I appreciated the sentiment, but I was also keen to challenge it a little further.

"Really, Mel? I mean, that's nice and all, and I want to believe it. I really do. But in the real world, it's guys like that who get ahead."

"I disagree," Mel replied with a firm headshake. She sat up a little taller in her seat.

"You do?" I pressed.

"Declan, if you want to really be successful as a reporter, or even life in general, if we're going to get all philosophical about it, there's only two words of advice you need to follow."

I leaned in closer. She had me hooked on her every word. As usual.

"Be you," she said with a friendly smile. "The world is full of entitled jackasses, but there's only one Declan Davies."

"Thanks," I said, feeling a little better.

"Now, I have an article due in T-minus one hour, so if you'll excuse me..."

And with that, she disappeared behind the cubicle wall. I could hear her put her headphones on and start tapping away furiously at the keyboard.

I set up a little taller and reached around, massaging around the pain in my lower back.

Today had been quite an interesting and very unexpected day.

Sometimes it really was better not to meet your heroes.

While other times, the people who you tried to avoid just showed up anyway and left you feeling...all sorts of weird ways inside.

Despite all the unforeseen twists and turns the day had taken, I remained crystal clear on one thing—I was officially banning myself from any more day drinking.

CHAPTER FIVE

PORTER

"What's up, bitches?!"

Before I knew what was happening, my nostrils were filled with the smell of strawberry bubblegum, and I had a princess party hat slapped onto my head and a green jello shot shoved into my hand.

"Hey, Nick," I said, managing a smile while quickly moving to take the princess party hat *off* my head.

Steel showed up a few exasperated steps behind his boy. Nick, meanwhile, was already off, assaulting—I mean, welcoming—the next people in through the doors.

It was the official grand opening of Steel's bar, *Deffers*, so I guess it was to be expected that Nick was feeling the hype.

"He called me 'bitches,'" I said in disbelief as I pulled Steel in for a hug.

He grabbed me by my elbows and looked at me. "That's just what he says. Don't take it the wrong way, Porter."

I tried to hide my annoyed scowl. Steel scanned my face and continued, "He means it in the non-offensive, playful, Britney Spears kind of way, not in the problematic, misogynistic way."

I *hmpfed* as vociferously as I could, wanting to make sure he heard it over the din of music and people laughing and chatting all around us.

I was equally confused as to why he had called me 'bitches', as in plural, since there was only one of me. Had I missed something? Was that how young people spoke these days? Was I officially becoming old?

"Just relax, will you?" Steel said, playfully elbowing me in the ribs. "And welcome to the grand opening of my bar!"

I shuffled my shoulders and loosened my stiff neck. "I am relaxing...bitches," I said with a ballsy smile.

I looked over at Steel for a moment.

The man looked genuinely happy—a little tired perhaps, but undeniably happy as well. He had a lot on his plate. He ran a successful law firm, Nick was proving to be a double handful, and he was now the silent partner of Daylesford's hottest new gay bar.

"Congratulations, my friend." I patted him on the shoulder.

He beamed as he looked around the place.

His place.

It was remarkable, the turnaround he had managed to achieve in just four short months. The place had formerly been a dive bar, and that was putting it generously. Gross flooring, a bad layout, horrendous lighting and, worst of all, a clientele of obnoxious millennial hipsters.

But now, the place had been completely transformed. Steel had hired the best interior design firm in the city, and it showed. Gone was the open-plan mess of nothing, and in its place were cozy, seperate areas, each with their own distinct, ambient feel. Perfect for socializing with old friends...as well as making new ones.

The long bar in the center of the space had been replaced by two smaller bars at each end. And gone were all the annoying pieces of furniture—all lacking proper back support—replaced instead with plush leather sofas and chairs that you could actually sit in...comfortably.

Yep, I was officially old.

The whole place was all very Zen Shui...or whatever it's called.

But as I looked around, the thing that warmed my heart the most was the people I saw. An eclectic bunch for sure, but definitely skewing predominantly toward the Daddy and boy types.

It felt like I was...home.

Ever since The Laird had become a no-go zone because it was owned by Mikey's douchebag ex-boyfriend, we had been out in the nightlife wilderness, struggling to find a bar that could make four Daddies, and now their three boys, feel relaxed and like they belonged.

That was exactly what Steel had managed to accomplish with the place. It was stylish, elegant, and laid-back, and it was going to be the hottest spot in town, judging by how busy it was.

"Great turnout," I said to Steel, who was still taking it all in.

"Tell me about it," he said. "Nick and Mikey did a great job getting the word out. We've even got press coming."

I must have rolled my eyes without realizing it because Steel scrunched up his eyebrows and looked at me strangely. Before I could delve into the details of *that* shit-show, I felt a gentle tap on my shoulder.

I turned around, and Mikey practically leaped into my arms. Well, he did leap into my arms, but he was so light that it felt like throwing on a warm blanket on a cold winter's night.

Once Mikey had moved on to Steel, Stirling gave me a close hug, too.

"It's good to see you both," I said. Mikey leaned into Stirling's large frame and the man instinctively wrapped an arm around his boy. They were both glowing. Almost a year and a half into their relationship and they were still clearly in their honeymoon phase.

I couldn't have been happier for them both. But for just the teeny-tiniest moment, I felt a brief flash of...I didn't know what. It was unfamiliar, almost like a longing for something.

"Good to see you too, Porter," Stirling said in his deep voice.

"Is Nick around?" Mikey asked Steel.

He nodded and pointed in the direction of a group of men Nick had walked up to. He held out a tray of shots and must have said something funny because the group erupted in laughter.

"Do you mind if I go and say hello, Daddy?" Mikey batted his gorgeous blue eyes at Stirling and there was no way the man could resist.

"Of course, baby."

And with a sweet kiss on the forehead, Mikey walked over to Nick, leaving the three of us standing together.

"How come Nick is working the event?" I asked.

"His choice," Steel replied with a shrug. "He was so excited about it and wanted to be involved..."

"But with clothes *on*," Stirling wryly observed.

I smiled. I liked Stirling. He was always the quiet one of the group, and even though he had opened up a lot more since he had been with Mikey, he was still more of a quality over quantity kind of guy when it came to speaking. It was one of my favorite things about him.

"It's a shame Hudson couldn't make it back," I said as another fully clothed waiter walked past us, and we each grabbed a drink off the tray he was carrying.

"It is," Steel said, bringing the beer to his mouth. "I think they're at some conference in Vermont... Should we sit?"

Stirling and I nodded in agreement. We followed Steel as he led us to the closed-off VIP section. It was dimly lit and a lot quieter than the main floor. We walked over to a table by the far wall and sat down.

"Well, cheers." I raised my glass. "Even though Hudson's not here, I know he's here in spirit, and from all three of us, Steel, we are so proud of you. This place is going to be the hottest Daddy bar in town."

"Hear, hear," Stirling concurred as we clinked our glasses together.

"Thanks, you guys." The pride was unmissable in Steel's voice.

We sat in silence with our drinks for a moment before Steel's light blue eyes focused in on me. "Why did you react funny when I said that the press was going to be here before, Porter?"

"It's nothing." I sighed into my drink.

I looked up and could see Stirling and Steel silently eyeing each other.

"*What's* nothing?" Stirling asked in that deceptively gentle yet firm way of his.

"Let's just say I'm not a huge fan of the media at the moment."

"Oh, of course," Steel said, slapping his forehead with his palm. "The sex scandal."

"Mayor Willy's Willy," Stirling added unhelpfully.

I shot them both an *I don't want to talk about it look*...which they both ignored.

"How's it all going?" Steel looked at me, and I could see the genuine worry in his eyes.

"It's going," I replied, trying not to show how disgruntled and out of sorts I was about the whole damn thing.

"Hey Steel." Nick's voice rang out as he rushed over to where we were sitting.

Steel looked up, and his face melted into a warm smile. "What is it, baby?"

"There's a reporter here, from *The Daylesford Times*. He wants to speak to you. He's just over there."

I looked to where Nick had pointed and couldn't believe what I saw.

Standing there, dressed in the second most ridiculous billowing suit I had seen that week and staring at the dancefloor like he was seeing one for the first time in his life, was none other than Mr. Declan Davies.

CHAPTER SIX

DECLAN

"Well, well, well. Look what we have here."

I turned my head in the direction of the smug voice and let out a small gasp.

"Porter. I mean, Mr. Porter. Shit, I mean, Mr. Jones."

Well, this had gotten off to a promising start.

Porter Jones walked up to me and greeted me with a firm slap on the back. Immediately, I had to turn away. I didn't want him seeing the pain he had unintentionally inflicted.

"Are you alright?" he asked, his voice laden with concern.

I took a deep breath and turned around to face him again. "I'm fine," I said through clenched teeth. The pain would be over soon. I just had to wait it out for a few more moments.

"Sorry, I didn't mean to startle you."

"That's okay," I said, my body starting to return to something resembling normality.

"Before we go any further," he said as he closed the space

between us, "perhaps we should agree on what we call each other? I'm happy with first names, if you are, Declan?"

"Yeah, that's fine."

I didn't know where to look. As much as my eyes wanted to stare at him, I also wanted to keep them away from him as long as possible. The man had a curious effect on me.

I looked down at my empty drink. He must have noticed it, too, because he asked, "Can I get you another one?"

I lifted my face to meet his gaze. "Uh, sure. Vodka soda, please."

"I'll be right back."

He grabbed my arm, and the touch spread a searing warmth throughout my entire body. "Don't move."

I might have been physically still, but my mind was racing at a million miles a minute. I didn't know how he did it, but somehow, Porter managed to bring up so many conflicting feelings all at once that it gave me whiplash trying to figure them out.

He went from smug to nice to arrogant to professional in a heartbeat.

Was he doing it on purpose? He did seem to enjoy psyching me out. Trying to intimidate me into telling him what he wanted to find out from me. Or was it just how the man operated? He was in politics, after all. Power plays and manipulating people to get ahead was all in a day's work for him. I assumed.

Porter returned with two drinks and handed me one. A wide smile stretched his lips, and he was just about to say something when an older, gray-haired man walked past. "Porter Jones," he said. "How great to see you."

"Councilor Young." Porter's smile froze on his face as his eyes darted frantically between me and the councilor. "How are you?"

"I'm good. Listen, I need to talk to you about that development on Fifth and Main. Have you got a moment?"

Porter looked back at me, and for a second, I could have sworn it looked like he didn't want to leave.

I smiled and gave him a friendly wave. "We can talk later...Porter."

The man wrapped his arm around Porter's shoulder and scuttled him away.

Great. It left me standing here alone, uncomfortable and more than just slightly pissed that I was back to covering things like the opening of some new club.

I hadn't been able to build any momentum since the mayor's selfie scandal. I sighed into my drink as I walked around, trying to find the owner of the place to get a quote for my article.

But my eyes never drifted far from Porter. He was dressed in tight-fitting black pants that looked like they were painted on to his well-defined legs and an olive green shirt that offset his skin color beautifully and brought out an emerald sparkle in his green eyes. It also hugged every tight muscle on his arms and torso in the most wicked of ways. I wondered what it would feel like to run my soft fingers over his hard chest, down to his slim waist, and sink my fingers into that meaty ass.

As soon as Councilor Young started to walk away from him, I pounced, striding over to him. But before I could swoop back in, someone else approached and began talking his ear off. And it continued like that for the rest of the evening.

One mini-interview with the co-owner and four or five vodka sodas later, I decided to call it a night. Porter clearly didn't have time to talk to me, and for whatever reason, that made me feel really crappy.

Thankfully, I had caught an Uber over and not driven, so I fished my phone out of my pocket to order myself a ride back home.

"Hey there."

The smooth touch of Porter's fingers across the back of my hand stopped me in my tracks.

"Oh hey," I said, a little petulantly.

"Are you okay?" His brows pinched together as his eyes scanned my face.

"I'm fine," I said, pulling my hand away from his and returning to what I had been doing—ordering a ride home. Although when I looked down, the screen was kind of blurry. Hmm...my phone was six months old. Maybe it was time for a new one? They become obsolete so quickly these days.

"I'm sorry we got interrupted before," he said with a warm affection in his voice.

"Did we? I mean, are you? I mean..."

Shit. I had no idea what I was saying.

Suddenly, the room started to spin, and I stumbled over my feet and smack bang into Porter's conveniently outstretched hands.

He deftly caught me, and his firm hands around my arms felt good. *Very* good.

"I'm alright," I said as I struggled back onto my feet. "Just some...uneven flooring here. Which I'm going to be sure to include in my article. The people of Daylesford have a right to know," I said as I wagged my finger perilously close to his soft, pink lips.

A smile spread across Porter's face, and there it was—that googly-eyed, *should be wrong but really was oh so right*, breathtaking smile of his. I finally got to see it, up close and personal.

"I want a photo with you," I blurted out, and it was right at that moment that I realized I had probably had one drink too many. But it was too late. My brain and my mouth were ganging up on me again, robbing me of reason or even, I don't know, anything resembling a normal filter.

"Where's my phone? Oh my God, it's been stolen. Porter, I've been robbed," I cried in alarm.

"Declan," Porter said in a voice that calmed—and silenced—me straight away.

"What?" I breathed into him.

He looked down and gave my hand a gentle tap. "You're holding your phone."

I may have been buzzing with alcohol, but I was alert enough to feel the red-hot wave of embarrassment washing over my whole body, from head to toe.

Damn it.

Right at that moment, I added nighttime drinking onto my *I'm not doing this anymore* list, right next to day drinking.

I looked Porter straight in the eye and let out a helpless breath.

I was a mess. A fool. And I wouldn't have blamed him in the slightest if he'd walked off in disgust and left me there by myself.

Who was I kidding? I didn't have it in me to be a big time, ruthless reporter. That wasn't me or who I was. I was just a nice guy in an oversized suit who'd had one too many drinks.

To my astonishment, rather than turning away, Porter looked at me with a searing intensity that ignited my insides. He stretched out his arm and delicately ran the back of his index finger underneath my jaw.

"Do you need some help?" he asked.

There was no judgment or malice in his voice, only an undercurrent of sexy that was quickly pulling me in.

I nodded and whispered, "Yes."

"Would you like *me* to help you?"

Oh, fuck yeah. "Please," I said as I looked down at the shaky ground, my vision starting to blur again.

"Come with me."

Those were the last three words I remembered him saying, and then everything turned to black.

A ray of bright sunshine streamed into the room assaulting what had been, up until that point, my firmly shut eyes.

I blinked a few times, before grabbing the silk pillow I was resting on and covering it over my face. Wait, I didn't have silk pillows. Mine were those cheap cotton ones you picked up from the bargain bin.

Where the hell was I?

I peeked out from under the smooth pillow. I was in a very well-appointed bedroom. It looked like something straight out of an interior design magazine. And it was pretty much the size of my entire apartment.

I got up and slowly walked down a hallway filled with picture frames full of attractive, smiling people in all sorts of exotic locations. The hallway led to a bright and airy kitchen. Standing over the stove, with his back to me, was Porter. He was cooking.

He was cooking shirtless, and his pajama bottoms were so tight that they left little to the imagination. Porter's tight, round ass looked as inviting as the delicious smells that were coming from the cooktop.

"Oh, hello," he said as he turned around and saw me standing there looking like an out-of-place idiot in his kitchen. My eyes trailed down the hard ridges of his abs, before returning to his face.

"How did I end up here...with you?" I asked groggily.

"Don't worry," he said with a gentle laugh as he motioned for me to come over and sit at the table. "Nothing happened. You were just a little..."

"Drunk?" I said guiltily.

"Yeah, that and..."

Great, there was more.

"Clingy. You wouldn't tell me where you lived, so I couldn't take you home."

Oh god...it couldn't get any worse.

"And apparently, you really like my biceps."

"Huh? Your biceps?"

Another laugh escaped Porter's lips, and I noticed his cheeks were a little flushed.

"Yeah, you kept talking about how much you liked them. Kept touching them, too."

Correction: it could get worse. It just fucking did.

I rubbed my bleary eyes, trying to wipe the shame and stupidity away. "I am so sorry, Porter."

"Don't worry about it," he said, flashing me that incredibly wacky smile of his, and it did all sorts of delicious things to my insides.

He plated up what he'd been cooking and brought me a full plate of bacon, eggs, mushrooms, tomatoes, and toast. I looked down at the food as my stomach let out an almost deafening growl.

"Sounds like someone's hungry. Eat," he said, giving me a nod to get started. He didn't have to tell me twice. I ate like I hadn't eaten all week, and it wasn't until the seventh or eighth mouthful that I began to feel like something resembling a human being again.

The whole time I was scarfing down food like a madman, Porter was resting against the sink, looking at me. There was a lightness to him that I had never noticed before.

"What? What is it?" I asked self-consciously.

"Nothing, sorry," he said as he turned around and busied himself with tidying up the countertop.

I finished chewing, stood up, and walked over to him.

"Why were you looking at me? Tell me."

His shoulders pinched up to his ears, and he turned around as slowly as was humanly possible.

"I didn't mean to creep you out," he began. "It's just that the light was coming into the kitchen, and with the way it was hitting your face and lighting up your eyes..."

I moved in a step closer to him.

"You're very attractive, Declan." His voice was barely more than a murmur.

I took another step closer to him.

"I think you're the most beautiful..."

And then I did the stupidest thing in the world. For some inexplicable reason, I turned my gaze from Porter's hypnotizing light green eyes and glanced over at the microwave. My eyes popped out of their sockets.

"Holy shit, it's ten to nine. I am soooo late. I have to go, Porter."

I rushed out of the kitchen and down the hall to the room I had slept in. I could hear Porter's footsteps close behind me. I stepped into the room, and my face fell as I looked at my crumpled clothes from the day before, lying in a heap on the floor.

"Fuck," I said as I dropped to my knees and tried to smooth them out with my hands.

"Declan."

I turned to look up at Porter.

"Relax. I'll order a car to pick you up. How about you jump in the shower and get ready?"

I stood up.

"That sounds good, thanks. Wait," I said, tugging on his arm, "what about clothes? I don't have anything to wear."

"I'll lend you something of mine," he said reassuringly.

"But I don't think we're the same size, Porter."

Porter leaned in so close to me I could feel his minty-fresh breath on my face. His lips stretched wide, and his eyes bulged out unevenly.

"And since when have you cared about wearing clothes that actually fit you, Declan?"

CHAPTER SEVEN

PORTER

Declan's unexpected stay overnight at my house meant that I was late to work too.

But what was I supposed to do? The guy had basically passed out right on top of me at the bar, and I couldn't get anything intelligible out of him, such as his address. Taking him back to my place and letting him sleep in my guest suite was the safest option.

I wasn't surprised he couldn't remember anything the next day. The only conversation he managed in the car ride on the way back from the bar was about my biceps, which it turns out he had developed—and shared—a very strong opinion about. Apparently, he liked them a lot and wanted to know what they would feel like wrapped around him.

If he hadn't been blind drunk, I would have pulled over right there and then and given him the fucking that he wanted so badly.

But he was, so I didn't.

I was perfectly gentlemanly as I put him to bed.

And I was equally as considerate in making him a big, hearty breakfast the next morning. Sure, I may have accidentally on purpose forgotten to put on a shirt, but I needed to test my theory out. I wanted to see whether Declan liked me, or at least my body, in a state of sobriety as much as he did after five drinks.

Turned out, he did. At least, if the way he kept staring at me was any indication.

I smiled at the thought of Declan liking me as I felt a rising heat spread out across my chest. I tugged at the collar of my crisp white business shirt. It was suddenly feeling a little tight.

"You're late," my assistant, James, snapped in his usual sassy, slightly campy voice as I strode into the office.

"And you look like you accidentally sat on a twelve-inch dildo. Good morning to you, too," I shot back with a cocky grin.

James had been my assistant for six years. He was in the lifestyle, too, but we never blurred the boundaries. We did like to rib each other every once in a while, though. "What's up your ass this morning?" I asked.

James lifted a perfectly sculpted eyebrow and dropped his head in the direction of my office door. "He's in there."

Fuck.

"And he's pissed."

Double fuck.

The willy scandal showed no signs of going down. Okay, bad choice of words. It showed no signs of ending.

The media was still covering it, almost a week and a half later. It was unheard of, and we were starting to take a hit in the polls. That would have been bad at any time, but in an election year, it was an unmitigated disaster.

"Thanks for the heads up," I said as I opened the door to my office, bracing for the fury that awaited me.

"I want an update, Porter," William said before I had even closed the door.

He was sitting in my chair with his feet on my desk. "It's been ten days." He dropped his feet heavily to the floor and rolled himself in, leaning over the desk. "Why the hell is this still front-page news? You were meant to take care of it."

"I am taking care of it." I didn't like the sound of my voice. It lacked the usual sheen and polish I could normally switch on in an instant.

And I knew why.

Or rather, I knew who.

Declan had distracted me.

Hmm, maybe that was *his* plan? Maybe his whole deer-in-headlights, *I can't handle more than a few drinks* schtick was just that—a routine to suck me in, lower my defenses, and be able to outplay and outmaneuver me.

I banished that thought from my mind. No, that didn't feel right. That wasn't what it was. It couldn't be. I didn't know what the hell Declan's deal was, but I knew he wasn't some master manipulator. And that was a good thing. The warm feeling returned to my chest. Maybe it was reflux? Damn, I had just turned forty, after all. I made a mental note to stop by the pharmacy on the way back home.

"I'm working on it, William," I said, throwing him a little shady side-eye as I sat down at my desk, in the guest chair.

"If this keeps going, Porter..."

His voice trailed off, but I knew exactly where he was going.

He was in trouble. While he had built up a lot of political capital over his decade and a half career, things in politics could change dramatically overnight. And the worst thing would be...

"If the resignation rumors start, I'm a goner," he said glumly.

The dreaded R-word.

It was pretty much the only thing a politician couldn't come back from, because once resignation rumors started swirling, they took on a life of their own. The momentum became unstoppable, and when it collided with cancel culture online, you were well and truly done.

Toast.

Finished.

Over.

It wasn't fair, and it wasn't right, but that's just the way things were.

"It won't get to that, William. I'll make sure of it."

"Will you?" He tilted his head to the side and let out a scoff. "It's no secret you want my job, Porter."

"What's that supposed to mean?" A hot anger curled in my gut as I stared the man down.

I could see him breathing heavier, his nostrils flaring. "Well, this plays beautifully into your hand, doesn't it? The mayor gets sideswiped by a sex scandal, paving the way for..."

"Don't even finish that sentence, William." I practically barked the words. "How fucking dare you. I have been nothing but loyal and worked my ass off for you, *for years*, and this is the thanks I get."

Yes, I wanted the top job, *his* job, but never like this. Not in a million years like this.

I wouldn't ever do anything so underhanded and awful to somebody else, and I would never, ever do anything that sex-shamed another person. That went against every fiber of my being.

He looked like he wanted to say something else, but he managed to stop himself at the last minute. Instead, he pushed himself away from the desk and stood up. He turned his gaze to the floor as he spoke, almost timidly, "I'm sorry, Porter. I shouldn't have said that. It's just..."

It looked as if his legs were about to give way, and he flung himself back down into the chair. "This is really hurting Peggy, which means it's really fucking killing me."

Pain washed over his face, and I genuinely felt bad for the man.

"I know it is," I said.

But I didn't.

I couldn't even begin to imagine the horror I would feel if I ever had any aspect of my sex life exposed so publicly the way he had.

That was my number one biggest fear in life and the reason why I kept my private life and my public persona so distinctly separate.

"I'm doing everything I can to sort this out," I added.

"Thank you."

The crack in his voice tore at my heart.

"Sorry, I'm in your seat."

He got up and walked around the table as I moved into my chair. I could see the toll the scandal was taking on him. The dark circles under his eyes, the slumped shoulders, the dejected way he walked the few steps around my desk.

"We'll get through this," I said as I sat down in the chair.

I had an innate self-confidence that I had been building up ever since the day my parents kicked me out of my own home. Every little challenge life threw at me, I used it to propel me forward and make me stronger. I wasn't about to let the mayor take a fall and lose his entire political career over a few private, intimate photos.

I may not have always liked the man, and I did want his job, but this wasn't right. And despite whatever...feelings I may have been having for Declan, nothing changed that simple fact. No one deserved to be exposed for anything they did behind closed doors. Or on their camera phones.

I searched my brain, trying to come up with a solution to get us out of this mess and to move the media onto something else.

Anything else.

The only thing my thoughts kept coming back to over and over again was Declan. I had to find out who the source of the story was, and I had to know what else he knew. Did he know, or was he able to find out, about William's other fetish? It was more important than ever.

I couldn't allow myself to get distracted by how cute he looked in an oversized suit.

Or how I imagined his body underneath it.

Or how relieved he looked whenever I offered to help him or came to his aid in any small way.

Or the way his eyes dragged up and down my shirtless body, his hunger and want clearly evident, without him even saying so much as a word to acknowledge it.

No, I needed to push all those sexy, distracting thoughts out of my head. I had to be at the top of my game to quash this story and make sure there was nothing coming down the pipeline that could hurt us in the coming months. And the only way to do that was to get the upper hand on Declan Davies.

"Oh, by the way, *The Daylesford Times* just confirmed the behind-the-scenes story we've been chasing for a while now," William said, breaking the silence that had fallen between us.

"Do you think that's a good idea?" I shot him a concerned look.

The story had actually been my idea a few months back. I thought that a puff piece on the mayor, following him around as he did all sorts of wonderful things—visiting sick children at the hospital, serving food at the homeless shelter—would serve to show him in a good light going into the election.

But with this seemingly never-ending willy story dragging on into its second week, we had to recalibrate. We wouldn't be in control of the article they published, so we had to tread very, very carefully.

"I did think of that," he said, squirming a little in his chair. "Which is why I've decided that the story will be about *you*."

"Me?" I sputtered.

He nodded, somewhat uncomfortably. "I'm a target at the moment, Porter. If they followed me around, the only thing they would want to focus on is the story."

That part I agreed with.

"So, you're essentially my next of kin."

My brows pinched together. He took a glimpse of the befuddled look on my face and continued to explain.

"You're close enough to me that any good news that you generate rubs off onto me by association. And if things continue the way they're going...well, let's just say it wouldn't hurt you to get some good publicity yourself."

The implication of what he was saying hit me like a ton of ambition-filled bricks. I sank into my chair. If this scandal kept going, and the mayor really did have to resign, that would be the opening I had been waiting for.

So many conflicting emotions whirred around in my brain.

"So, you'll do it, then? You'll have a reporter follow you around for a few weeks, seeing you in the best possible light, doing all the things I was meant to be doing, basically?"

"Uh, sure." My mind was unable to focus on any one thing. There was so much racing through it, so many things to consider.

Was this really my chance?

No, I reminded myself. This wasn't the right time, and this wasn't about me. My top priority was to protect the mayor. That was my job, and it was the right thing to do. My personal ambitions would have to wait for a more appropriate opportunity.

"Good," William said with a half-smile as he stood up. "I'm glad that's all sorted."

He took out a piece of paper from his inside jacket pocket and handed it to me. "That's got the name and details of the reporter who's been assigned to the story."

I nodded vacantly as the mayor left my office.

I reached for my phone. I hadn't been sticking to my daily meditation routine very well, and right now, I needed some fucking zen. Stat.

As I opened the app on my phone, my eyes glanced over to the paper William had given me. I blinked as I stared at it in disbelief.

The reporter who had been assigned to the story was none other than one Declan Davies.

CHAPTER EIGHT

DECLAN

"Are you kidding me? That's a great story to land." Mel's face buzzed with excitement, while mine was still frozen, suspended in shell-shocked disbelief.

"Is it, though?" I asked, looking across at her smiling face peering over at me.

She nodded so hard the whole cubicle divider shook.

"Yes, it is. Everyone knows that the chief of staff wants to be Daylesford's next mayor. And you're the one getting exclusive, behind-the-scenes access to him."

I didn't know about that. The briefing with Carmen, our editor, had been short, but very specific. This was a puff piece, which was basically just one rung beneath an all-out promotional, sponsored piece.

I wouldn't be getting the chance to flex my investigative muscles. No, I was going to follow Porter Jones around as he presented a carefully constructed, fit-for-public consumption view of himself. An image that, by and large, he would be in charge of, and I would be left to write up. I could see it now. Library openings, volunteer work, his reading lists that showed how smart and cultured he was, all designed to give the impression that the man, besides looking like a fucking *GQ* cover model and who could cook a mean-ass breakfast, also just so happened to live the life of a male version of Mother Teresa.

"Besides," Mel said as her eyes went all dreamy, "have you seen him? The man is a hunk machine of sexiness."

I laughed. "Maybe that should be the headline?"

"Hey, don't steal my ideas," Mel teased, wagging her brightly painted, fluro-blue fingernails my way.

"You can see he's attractive, though, right?"

Uh yeah, I did have eyes. Hello.

"He's...okay." I gave a one-shoulder shrug, hoping to conceal the flash of heat coursing through my body. The only thing more mind-blowingly insane than how crazy-hot Porter was, was that he seemed to think that I was attractive too. Beautiful, even. Unless I had misheard what I had heard him say—or what he was about to say before I stupidly interrupted him—in his kitchen. Yeah, I must have been in some hangover haze and imagined the whole thing. There was no way someone like him would be interested in someone like me.

I had no clue how he was able to do it, but Porter Jones did *something* to me that made me feel things I had never felt before. And that was freaking scary.

I had only ever had one long-term relationship before, and it was enough to put me off men for good. John started off as a nice guy, but as I learned a few months in, it was all an act. He committed the cardinal sin that no Dom should ever commit: he didn't respect my limits.

I had been badly burned dipping my toe into the kink lifestyle, and I was never going to make the same mistake again. I may have been young, but I wasn't stupid. Doms simply couldn't be trusted. I had learned that lesson big time.

I didn't know why my thoughts about Porter had led me to think about John, which in turn made me think about...*that* sort of stuff. Porter was becoming way too good at scrambling my thoughts and leaving me feeling...confused, yet slightly aroused at the same time.

I cleared my throat and looked up at Mel. "I'm a professional, Mel. How Porter Jones looks doesn't affect anything, least of all my approach to this story."

"I wasn't doubting that for a minute," she said with an effervescence that suggested she was enjoying this a little more than she should have been. "I'm just saying he's an attractive man, that's all. There's no harm in appreciating that, Declan."

"Yeah, I guess so."

She was just stating the blatantly obvious, after all. Porter was a good-looking guy, so it was only natural that he would elicit a response in me. I was just appreciating his attractiveness and nothing else. Yeah, that was it.

"When's your first meetup with him?" she asked.

"This afternoon. At his place."

She quirked an eyebrow as her bright pink lips stretched into a grin. "His place?"

"Yeah," I said absently. "He's got a really nice house."

Our eyes locked. "Apparently."

Before her wide grin could morph into a line of questioning I was desperate to avoid, I quickly added, "It's a good starting point, to see him at home and start to build a relationship with him."

"A *professional* relationship, or..." Her words lingered, leaving an uneasy edge in the air between us.

"Well, have fun," she said breezily as she slid down into her seat and out of view.

Fun? I wasn't going to his place for that.

I cringed as the memory of waking up at his house came

flooding back. And that memory was quickly joined by the spectacle I had made of myself at the bar the night before and the fool I must have looked like in the boardroom at our first meeting.

I swung back in my seat and looked up at the ceiling. What on earth must the man have thought about me?

Fun was the last thing on my mind.

No, for the next few weeks, I was going to be the most focused and professional I had ever been in my life.

I was going to show Porter Jones that I was one serious reporter.

"Please come in." Porter's maid smiled warmly as she held the wood-paneled front door open for me and ushered me in. "Mr. Jones is out in the back, if you'd like to follow me."

"Sure, thank you."

I hadn't seen much of his house during my first...visit. But what I was seeing now was just as impressive as I remembered his kitchen and guest bedroom being. The man clearly had good taste, as well as the money, to afford a huge house in one of the nicest suburbs in Daylesford.

The overall decor was masculine, filled with hues of brown and copper, with plenty of earthy elements, like a sheepskin rug by the fireplace or a wall of greystone that I caught a glimpse of as we walked past the study.

"He's in the pool," the maid said as she led me outside.

The backyard was impressively large and landscaped in a more traditional, formal style than the inside of the house. It looked like the 'after' shot on one of those gardening redesign shows.

I could hear the sound of water splashing as I looked over to the large rectangular pool.

"I'll leave you to it," the maid said as she turned and went back into the house.

"Thank you," I replied as I walked over to the gigantic aqua pool. I leaned against the glass pool fence and watched as Porter's arms and feet splashed through the water as he swam. He was a good swimmer—fast, too.

I used the momentary reprieve to compose myself.

Focused and professional, that was what I was going to be. We might have gotten off on a slightly unsteady, margarita-induced footing, but I was determined to change all of that.

The sounds of swimming stopped.

I turned my attention to the pool just as Porter was stepping out. His fingers gripped the stainless steel sides of the pool ladder, and his shoulders flexed as he lifted himself out of the water, one dripping wet, mouthwatering step at a time. His hair shone in the afternoon sunlight and his entire torso glistened, beaded with golden gems of water.

As more of his body came into view, my eyes widened when they landed on the swimming trunks he was wearing. Or was that a handkerchief? Because it was seriously the smallest swimsuit known to humankind.

A flimsy piece of navy blue fabric sat low on the man's hips. The drawstring was actually cut into the design—revealing a glimpse of pubic hair sticking out ever so teasingly, the culmination of a golden trail that began just below his belly button.

When I managed to draw my eyes up his body and to his face, my heart fluttered so hard in my chest I had to tighten my grip on the pool fence to remain upright.

That smile.

That goofy, asymmetrical smile of his got me.

Every.

Single.

Time.

He grabbed a towel and began drying his hair off as he walked over to me.

"Good to see you again, Declan," he said, wrapping the towel around his waist, not bothering to dry off his still-slick chest.

"Nice to see you too, Porter." My voice cracked as if it was breaking for the second time in my life.

If Porter's not-so-subtle attempts at seduction were a boxing match, he had won the first round.

But the fight wasn't over just yet.

Conveniently timing a midafternoon swim so that he could come out and greet me practically naked showed me that the man didn't play fair. I'd have to play dirty, too...and for some reason, that thought sent a powerful thrill through me.

"Can I get you anything to drink?" he asked as he walked over to the bar area beside the pool. Because of course he had a bar next to his pool.

"No, thanks," I said politely, but firmly. "I've sworn off day drinking."

He bent over to open up the mini-fridge behind the bar. I strained my head and peered over, sneaking a peek at his ass. The only thing separating me from it was a thin towel and a barely-there thread of nylon and spandex.

"Maybe I will have a drink," I cried out. "Just one."

It couldn't hurt, right?

He stood up with two beers in hand and motioned for me to follow him to the row of deck chairs on the other side of the pool.

I kept my gaze on the ground as I followed him, not looking up to see his broad, sculpted shoulders, or his biceps, which were flexing as he carried the drinks, or his ass that seemed to be inviting me as it moved temptingly under his towel with every step he took.

We reached the deck chairs and he handed me the drink. He unpeeled the towel from his hips and lay down, looking like the Grecian statue that he was. His body was all hard lines, firm ridges, and tight, compact muscles. And skin, all that glorious sun-tanned and still-dripping-wet skin.

I sat gingerly on the edge of the deck chair beside him, hardening in my resolve to stay completely professional and ignore his blatant attempts at trying to distract me with his distractingly amazing body.

"Do you swim a lot?" I asked after taking the first swig of beer, the cold liquid feeling good against the back of my dry throat.

"Every day, if I can," Porter said, bringing his hands behind his head. His biceps bulged even more, framing his strong, angular face perfectly. I looked away.

"How about you?" he asked.

"I used to love it as a kid, but not anymore."

"Why's that?"

I turned to look at him. The expression on his face indicated that he was genuinely curious to know why.

"I—I don't know," I lied.

I took another swig of beer and racked my brain, trying to find another topic to move on to. But Porter wasn't about to let it go.

"Well, there's no time like the present."

And with that, he leapt to his feet and peered down at me with an expectant look on his face.

"Uh, no. I am *not* going in for a swim, Porter." I couldn't believe this guy. Was he for real?

He tilted his head to the side with all the charming innocence of someone who knew exactly what they were doing. "Why not? The water's nice and warm."

Something in the low, suggestive way he said it hummed blissfully in my chest.

"Are you wearing underwear?" he asked.

"Of course I am."

That dopily adorable smile broke out across his face again. My heart thundered in my chest.

"Is it white?"

"What, my underwear? No," I said.

"Then you're all set."

And with that, he turned on his feet and did a perfect, head-first dive into the pool, barely making a splash.

When he reappeared at the side of the pool a few moments later, the smile was still firmly lodged on his face. He swam back a little away from the edge, and the next thing I knew, he started flicking water at me.

"Hey, quit it!" I yelled as I ducked to move out of the way. "That's very immature, Porter."

"Then why are you laughing?"

Was I?

Shit, I was.

"Come on, just one little swim, and then we can get down to business."

I stood up and looked down at myself. I hadn't done a very good job of avoiding the torrent of water he had sent my way, so I was half wet already.

But to go for a swim?

With him?

With...my body?

The panic rose up my body, my heartbeat now pounding in my head like a bomb ticking, about to go off. The last person who had seen my body was John. In our last argument, he had called me an unfuckable freak.

"I'll let you ask me anything." Porter's playful voice rang out and momentarily pushed the panic away.

I looked at him, swimming around in the pool, so light and joyous and drop-dead gorgeous.

With a shaky finger, I began to unbutton my shirt.

Porter swam back to the edge of the pool. I could feel the searing heat of his gaze boring into me. I lifted the shirt off my shoulders and tossed it onto the deck chair behind me.

I sat down, hurriedly taking off my socks and shoes. I got back up and unzipped my pants with trembling fingers.

He would see.

And he'd hate it.

Just as much as I fucking did.

I was scared.

I took a few steps toward the pool.

His eyes never left me.

I had carried the shame over how I looked ever since I was twelve and had started to develop back pain and debilitating headaches. The tests revealed that I had idiopathic scoliosis. It wasn't hereditary. In fact, no one knew how I got it or even what caused it.

From that moment on, something that I had taken for granted—a normal-looking spine—became the thing I wanted more than anything else in the world, as my back began to bend and curve slightly more each year as I got older. Mom worked jobs that didn't have health insurance, and there was no way she could afford the expensive surgery that was needed, so I only had one choice: live with it.

It was something that many people did live with, but in my case, the scoliosis came as a package deal with a number of related connective tissue disorders. That meant one thing: constant pain. Over the years, it had spread up to my neck and shoulders. Even my legs would hurt and easily cramp up if I ever did anything too strenuous.

But, again, something I had no choice but to live with.

In my everyday life, I could hide the way my spine curved to the left, especially when wearing a suit that was much too large for me.

But in just my underwear? It was noticeable, unavoidable...and downright hideous. John was right. I was an unfuckable freak.

I reached the pool and dipped my foot in. Porter was right, the water was invitingly warm.

I looked over at him, and that's the moment it happened. His sparkling green eyes drifted from my face and onto my back.

He saw it.

There was no way he couldn't see it.

And now, there was no way he could un-see the gross monster I was.

"Do you still want me to come in?" I asked so quietly it sounded more like a whisper.

"Of course," he said as he paddled over to where I was standing in a few short strokes.

"Can I help you?" he asked as he outstretched his two golden-tanned arms toward me.

I was taken aback and had to remind myself to keep breathing. Surely, this was a mistake? Why was he doing this? I looked at him, and he seemed completely fine. Normal. As if he wasn't bothered in the slightest by my appearance.

He helped me lower myself down the steps until I was fully submerged in the water.

"There you go," he said with a grin. "It's not so bad now, is it?"

Not bad? It felt amazing.

I swam away from him, letting the warm water loosen my muscles and work its restorative magic all over my body. I hadn't gone swimming in years, and it felt absolutely heavenly. The weightlessness of the water seemed to suck the pain out of me, allowing me to float aimlessly and, for the first time since I could remember, with a whole lot less pain.

Porter drifted over to me and I felt his hands grab my waist. My feet touched the tiles at the bottom of the pool and I allowed him to pull me into him in one steady, firm movement.

Our chests collided underwater, but in a controlled, gentle way. I felt his hands gliding up my back with such a silky softness it made me soft...and hard...at the same time.

It was as if he knew it was exactly what I needed.

I didn't know what came over me, but the next thing I knew, I had my fingers pressed into his meaty ass cheeks. They were as delectably firm as they looked under the towel.

I brought my hands to the front and palmed his erection

underwater. The friction of my fingers against his trunks made his head fall back.

"That feels so good," he murmured, as the sunlight caught the faintest hint of stubble on his jawline.

He gently interlaced his fingers around the nape of my neck, bringing our faces together, our breath intermingling.

"Kiss me, Porter." The need in my voice was heavy, urgent.

"That's exactly what I intend on doing."

And with that, he brought his lips to mine, the sweetness surprising me in the best way possible. He pressed slightly firmer into the back of my neck, and I opened my mouth, letting him in.

His tongue was soft. He controlled it expertly as he carefully explored the inside of my mouth with such reverence it made my body ache for him. I kept my hand on his cock, squeezing it as I slid my fingers up and down its ever-increasing hardness.

"Mr. Porter," the maid called out. "You have a telephone call."

"Tell them I'm busy," Porter yelled as he pulled himself away from me.

"It's Mayor Smith," the maid shouted back.

"Fuck," Porter hissed. "I have to take it. I'm sorry, Declan," he said as he unlaced his fingers from around my neck and started swimming away from me.

Suddenly, the water felt like an icy lake in the middle of winter.

"Stay for dinner?" he said over his shoulder as he got out of the pool.

"Yeah...sure...okay."

Porter disappeared inside, and I got out of the pool. I walked over to the deck chairs and grabbed the towel he had left for me.

I began to dry myself off as I wondered who had won the pool round of seduction.

Was it Porter because he had gotten what he wanted—me in the pool with him?

Or was it me because I had gotten what I had wanted? The

man's arms wrapped around me. Plus, the added—and unexpected—bonus kiss.

Screw being professional and focused.

Kissing Porter Jones was way more fun.

The next few weeks were going to be very interesting indeed.

CHAPTER NINE

PORTER

The mayor's badly timed phone call should have been the shot in the arm I needed to wake up out of my Declan-inspired stupor.

Should have been...but wasn't.

I managed to put the call out of my head in no time and enjoyed spending the rest of the afternoon with Declan. Ostensibly, he was doing some background research on me for the article he was writing. So why did it feel so much more casual, more relaxed, like I was hanging out with a good friend?

It could have had something to do with the fact that, when he wasn't inebriated or looking like he was in over his head in his office-slash-boardroom, Declan Davies was actually a really cool guy.

"Oh crap," he winced as he dragged the pieces reluctantly along the board. "You own Park Place, *and* you've got two houses on it."

I smiled. An innocent game of Monopoly brought out an animated side to him. I liked it.

"I do," I said with a firm nod and using a stern voice. "And I'm afraid you owe me, Mr. Davies."

Declan was desperately fumbling around the few notes he had left on his side of the table. "Crappity crap, crap, crap. I'm going to have to sell something."

I leaned over and placed my hand on his fidgeting fingers. "Or you can, you know, negotiate. I might be...open to that."

Okay, maybe it wasn't such an innocent game, after all.

Declan looked up, and I could see the second he registered that my low tone meant I wasn't talking about how much he owed me for landing on my Park Place houses.

I saw his Adam's apple thrashing around madly in his throat, and then that deer-in-headlights look returned to his face again. All that was missing was his trademark hideous bargain basement suit. He looked much nicer wearing an old white shirt and gray sweatpants of mine. Granted, they sat baggy on him, but that seemed to be the look he was going for most of the time anyway.

Based on what I saw at the pool, it all started to make sense. The oversized clothes, why he jumped a mile when I had placed my hand on his shoulder at the bar, the look of sheer terror in his eyes when I asked him to join me for a swim.

One of my friends in high school had developed scoliosis. But she had gotten hers treated with surgery. Declan, for whatever reason, hadn't. I was keen to find out more. I wanted to know all of the details, but I wasn't going to press the matter any further either. I would let him tell me if and when he felt comfortable enough to.

"Shit, it's almost seven," he said, picking up his cell phone off the table.

"I wish you'd stop doing that," I said.

"Doing what?" His brows pinched together tightly.

"Looking at the time. Every time you do..."

His cheeks reddened as the words hung in the air between us.

I wasn't embarrassed by what I had said. I had meant every

word I told him that morning. And if he had let me finish, I would have said that he was the most beautiful boy I had ever laid eyes on.

There were two types of beauty in the world: the type you saw and the type that couldn't be seen.

I had been with my fair share of surface-level pretty boys. The ones that looked good on the outside—hard bodies, cute faces—but when you looked under the hood, so to speak, you'd find an empty wasteland. That wasn't necessarily a bad thing. Most times, I wouldn't even stick around long enough to look under the surface. Maybe there was more to them, but I was never interested.

But with Declan, it was different.

He was different.

He had the surface-level beauty thing down pat. He was stunningly gorgeous. I was reminded of that glaring fact every time I looked at him. I liked the way his thick, wavy hair fell onto his forehead, the smoothness of his skin, the slight groove in his chin.

I liked seeing his face transform. His natural expression had an edge to it—not full-on resting bitch face, it was more like resting concentration face. As if there was a world of thought running behind his hazel eyes. But when he smiled, his whole face lit up, radiating the most wonderful energy.

And I made a mental note of his full lower lip. I hadn't spent nearly enough time tasting it. That was something I needed to change, because I had a sneaking suspicion it would quickly become the latest addition to the growing list of things I liked about Declan Davies.

But one of his most alluring traits was his complete oblivion to just how stunning he really was. He was breathtakingly beautiful. Everyone in the world could see it. Well, everyone except for him.

So, for some illogical and unknown reason, I found myself inadvertently under his thrall without even trying. He had a way about him that made me long to know more. It was as if in some way, he had found the key to my door and could let himself in whenever he wanted to.

That should have unnerved me, at least a little. But it didn't. Instead, it made me want to do things like cook him breakfast, make sure he was safe, and, right about now, order some takeout and have dinner with him.

I slapped my hands on the table, startling him a little. "You hungry?"

He bit down on that full lower lip of his and nodded. He really had no idea how freaking cute he could be sometimes.

"I'll order some takeout. You like Thai?"

He hesitated. "Sure?"

"Why don't I believe you?" I said with a grin.

"Well, it's just..." I looked down and saw his fingers fidgeting with the Monopoly pieces.

"Just what?" I pressed lightly.

"I've never actually eaten Thai food before."

"Oh. Well, would you like to try? I can stick to the safe beginner options if you like."

I had no idea in that moment that I would be saying those exact same words to him one more time before the evening was over.

His sublime smile lit up his face, and he nodded enthusiastically. "Yes, please."

Half an hour later, I was laying out a beginner's Thai buffet on my kitchen table. I explained each of the dishes to Declan and then sat back in my seat, observing him as he began to fill his plate with food.

He was cautious at first, almost a little nervous. I noticed that whenever he was anxious, he tugged at his shirt sleeve. It was an involuntary movement, I didn't think he even knew that he was doing it.

We were eating and laughing away in no time, like we had been all afternoon. Time really does fly when you're having fun. I couldn't remember the last time I had felt this comfortable around someone new.

We were keeping the conversation casual and breezy. I was

doing my best to restrain myself and not move the conversation into any number of different topics that I was very keen to explore. I had to keep reminding myself that he was here for work, getting background information on me to flesh out the article he was writing.

"Can I ask you a question?"

"Sure," I answered. "Ask me anything."

"Really?"

I nodded my head.

"Can it be...off the record?"

I glanced over at him. His hazel eyes were glassy, and his face had taken on a seriousness I hadn't seen on his face before.

I wiped the corners of my mouth with the napkin. "I think we moved into off-the-record territory the moment you grabbed my cock in the pool."

His eyes widened a little.

A stunned silence ensued between us.

I wasn't worried, though.

The more time I spent with him, the more I began to understand that Declan Davies was someone I should never underestimate.

"Well, I heard a rumor about you." He cleared his throat before saying more. "It wasn't a very nice rumor."

"I'm all ears."

"It's of a...personal nature, and let me repeat that this is just a rumor."

"Declan," I said calmly, placing my hand over his. "Just tell me already."

"I heard you sleep around. A lot."

I pulled my hand back.

I wasn't expecting that. For the first time in my life, my sex life was colliding with my professional life, and I didn't like the unsettled feeling it created within me. My palms felt clammy and my mouth went dry.

"Who did you hear this rumor from?" I asked, keeping my voice as steady as I could.

Declan pursed his lips. "You know I can't tell you that, Porter."

I had to admire his persistence. Even though right at that moment, I freaking hated it.

I looked down at my half-eaten plate. When I looked back up at Declan, his face had softened. Something about the way he looked at me made me feel like I could tell him. Not everything, but at least a few things.

"This is strictly off-record, right?" I confirmed.

"Absolutely."

"I got kicked out of my home at seventeen for being gay."

Declan leaned in closer. "Oh my gosh, Porter, I'm so sorry. That must have been..."

"Fucking horrendous," I jumped in. "But in a way, something good came out of it."

Declan scrunched up his face as he looked at me intently, trying to understand what I was saying.

"I learned not to apologize for who I was. I figured the worst thing that could have happened had already happened: my family had rejected me and thrown me out onto the streets."

A searing look of pain fell across Declan's face.

"I am a highly sexual person, Declan. And I refuse to be defined by it—almost as much as I refuse to apologize for being who I am. And what I'm into."

"Into?"

That question ticked my heart rate up a notch.

Okay, now we were veering into very dangerous, *approaching-my-boundaries* territory. There was no way I could possibly tell him what I was truly into, but I wanted to at least give him a hint, an indication, of where I was coming from.

"People are into all sorts of things sexually," I began.

He shifted a little in his chair.

"Some people just like straight-up vanilla sex."

I looked over, and Declan's face was neutral.

"Others like exploring different things..."

Declan's face tightened; his eyes constricted.

"Like playing with toys. Or having multiple partners..."

I could see his chest heaving, but I continued.

"Or spanking, or rope play, or anything else that would fall under BDSM."

The word set something off in Declan. He let out a heavy exhalation and turned away from me.

"Are you alright, Declan?" I was worried. The last thing I wanted to do was make him uncomfortable.

"I'm fine," he said, turning back to look at me. He didn't sound or look fine at all. "Please, continue."

For a moment, I was speechless. I didn't know what to say. So I repeated my tried and true line. "I'm a highly sexual person. I don't see anything wrong with consenting adults exploring their desires, their fantasies. I refuse to apologize for not having any—"

"Morals?" Declan spat the word out.

"I was going to say hang-ups."

Clearly, he was triggered.

"Does talking about, let's just call it non-conventional sex bother you, Declan?"

"No," he replied, way too defensively. "I just don't get it, that's all."

"What's there to get?"

"What's wrong with plain old normal sex?" His words were masking pain, I could sense it.

"Nothing," I replied.

"Oh." It looked like he wasn't expecting that answer.

I went on.

"It's just that some people have a different view on what they consider normal. And others avoid normal like the plague. It all comes down to personal preference. As long as it's between consenting adults, I don't see anything wrong with what people choose to do sexually. Does that make sense?"

"Kinda," he relented.

He really was in some sort of heightened state. Was this conversation bringing something up for him? Had he been hurt by someone before?

We sat silent for a few moments.

He looked at me curiously. "What are you into?"

His question slammed straight into the wall of the firmest boundary I had ever set in my life. That part of me considered answering him, even for just the briefest of moments, set off an alarm bell in my chest.

"I, uh..." I scratched behind my neck, desperately searching for at least a semi-intelligible answer I could give him. "I'd—I'd rather not talk about that."

Declan wove his fingers into mine. "Well then, why don't you show me?"

I didn't know what my face was doing, but whatever it was elicited a sweet laugh out of Declan. "Completely off-record, of course," he added cheekily.

My mind was positively frantic as we got up and I led Declan by the hand to my bedroom.

What was he expecting?

What was happening here?

What was he thinking?

What did he want?

What did I want?

What was I feeling?

How much of myself was I prepared to reveal to him?

We stepped into the bedroom, and I still hadn't found a single answer to any of the questions buzzing around in my head. Thankfully, Declan pushed himself into my arms and his soft lips pressed against mine to distract me.

He certainly wasn't shy about touching me. His hands were all over my body, grazing my stomach, massaging my shoulders, grabbing my ass. His desire was pure, and yeah, it felt good being wanted by him.

He stiffened when I tried to lift his shirt off him.

"Is this okay?" I asked.

His eyes went stormy, flickering through a hundred different emotions. "Yes," he said softly. "But be gentle with me, please."

My heart melted at his words. There was nothing more I wanted to do in the world than be gentle with him and give him everything he needed.

I got him naked in no time, exercising all the care I could. I kept my eyes locked on him, searching for the tiniest sign of pain or discomfort, but there was none. I quickly slipped out of my clothes, too, and there we were, standing naked, face to face, our erections pressing up against each other's bodies.

He grabbed my cock and pulled at it. There was nothing gentle about it. Good thing I didn't mind a bit of pain once in a while. His lips crashed into mine as he ran his thumb over my cockhead, spreading the precum around and then using it as makeshift lube as his surprisingly strong fingers slid up and down my entire length. The sensation felt amazing. I nibbled down on his lower lip, never wanting to release it from my teeth.

"You wanted me to show you what I'm into?" I asked, somehow managing to pull myself away from his sweet lips.

"Uh-huh," he said, letting go of my cock and grabbing my hair, pulling it with a firmness I found intoxicating. "What have you got, Porter Jones?"

"Oh, I can show you so much, Declan Davies," I growled into his ear as I bit down on his lobe. "The question is, what are you ready for?"

He pulled away and, again, exhaled deeply and looked around the room, anywhere to avoid my eyes.

"Hey." I delicately hooked my fingers under his chin, tilting his head up. "I can stick to the safe beginner options, if you like," I said for the second time that night.

That brought a smile to his lips. With a firm nod, he added, "Thank you, Porter."

I was slightly taken aback. Why was he thanking me for simply doing the most basic of things, communicating clearly and setting—and respecting—some boundaries?

I walked him over to my bed, helping him to lie down.

"Are you comfortable?" I asked.

"Yes."

"Good. Then don't move."

I ducked into my en suite bathroom and reemerged a few seconds later.

"What's that?"

He moved himself upright and a little closer to the headboard, trying to get a better view of what I was holding.

I held out the black leather cuffs I was holding. "These are wrist cuffs," I said as I sat down on the bed next to him.

"Oh." He looked down.

"Have you seen these before?"

"Yes."

His answer surprised me. I was under the impression that he had zero experience with anything that wasn't *plain old normal sex*. But maybe I was wrong.

I studied his face, but he seemed strangely relaxed. I looked down the length of his lean body, and his cock had remained pleasantly hard.

"What are you going to do with me?" His body trembled as he spoke.

I ran my hand gently across his chest. "Whatever you want and feel good with."

He swallowed down and nodded. He reached his arm out and grazed my cheek with his fingertips. "How about you tell me first?"

I smiled. "Sure."

I raised the handcuffs so he could see them. "I'd like to put these on you. Two would be nice, but one is perfectly fine."

His fingers were now tracing the top of my thigh, and the ticklish sensation it produced spread a warm tingle throughout my entire body. I liked his touch. I wanted more of it.

"And then I'd like to please you. We don't have to fuck..."

"I want to." His words fell out of his mouth so quickly, he was just as taken aback as I was. "One restraint, though, please."

He was so polite. I loved it.

My cock twitched. It loved it too.

I did as he requested.

I walked over and pulled out an anchor point from under the corner of my bed.

"What's that?" he asked, his eyes glued to me.

"It's a strap. I have a number of these under the bed and behind the headboard. I'll attach this," I flapped the wrist restraint I was holding in my hand, "to your wrist, and then I'll strap your wrist into the anchor point. It will keep you steady and in place."

He swallowed a moan as a bead of precum oozed out of his cock slit. I loved seeing how excited my words were making him.

"And you'll be comfortable, too. I promise," I continued. "The wrist strap is made of nylon, so it's soft against your skin. We can also adjust it so that the firmness suits you too."

A smile flashed across his face, but he didn't say anything.

"I like to be prepared," I said, a little sheepishly as I suddenly realized how Dom-like I must have been coming across to him. "Speaking of which, even though we're only at beginner level, I think we should have a safeword."

Declan blinked at me a few times. "A safeword?"

"You know what that is, right?" I asked.

He nodded.

"It's important to me that we both feel safe and know that if anything happens, at any time, we can say the word, and I'll stop whatever is happening immediately."

Declan's full lower lip trembled. "You will?" he whispered, looking like he was suddenly overcome with emotion.

"Of course I will. Straightaway. You're safe with me, Declan."

He exhaled loudly again, but this time, it was like a wall had been broken, and relief spilled out of him.

"Thank you."

The softness of his words hit me straight in the heart.

"So, have you got a preference for a word?" I said.

"Calista Flockheart," he said without the slightest hesitation.

"Excuse me, what?" Where on earth did that come from?

"She's my least favorite actress of all time," Declan explained. "She was in Ally McBeal, remember?"

"Vaguely," I said. I'd never watched the show. "Look, Declan, *Calista Flockheart* is slightly long for a safeword. Plus, now that I've said it aloud, *Flockheart* sounds a little like *flog hard*. Not that that's what we're doing, but it could be a little...confusing."

Declan took what I said and looked like he was considering it very seriously.

"What about McBeal?" he asked.

"Sure, McBeal is the safeword. The moment I hear it, whatever is happening, I will stop it as quickly and safely as possible. Okay?"

He nodded.

"And Declan," I added. "I will never, ever be mad at you for using the safeword. Ever. In fact, I'll be happy that you did, okay?"

His eyes glazed over before a determined look took over his face.

"Thank you, Porter."

I grabbed condoms and lube from the bedside drawer, giving my cock a few quick tugs to get myself fully hard as I eyed his long, lithe body. It was just as I hoped it would be. Lean and muscly, but on the smaller side.

For some reason, I knew this would be different. I didn't know how, but I could just sense it. This wasn't some scene at Revolver or an anonymous app hookup.

No, you idiot. This is the guy who is writing an article about you and could potentially expose you and ruin your entire career.

I pushed that thought out of my mind as quickly as it had entered.

With all the care in the world, I took his right hand and placed the restraint around it. Gently, I clipped it into the anchor point with a soft click.

"How does that feel?" I asked straightaway.

Declan closed his eyes for a few moments, breathing heavily as he allowed himself to adjust to the sensation.

"Perfect," he finally said as he opened his eyes and beamed at me.

I greased my fingers with lube and gently pressed my index finger to his hole. His entrance twitched at the touch, making my own cock ache with an almost painful need.

I slowly eased my finger into him, my eyes roving his face, his body, looking for any signs of discomfort or pain. There weren't any. So, I added another slicked finger, this time eliciting a sharp hiss from him.

"How are you feeling, Declan?"

He took a moment to respond. "Good. *Sooo* good."

His words managed to make me even harder than I already was. I placed my swollen, lubed-up cock against his pink hole. His body jolted but then stopped. He looked over at the restraint on his right wrist and he let out a loud, needy groan.

"Fuck me, Porter." His voice was laden with need. "I want you inside of me. Now."

I didn't hesitate. I entered him, slowly and steadily, until I was fully inside of him. He felt so velvety smooth wrapped around my cock. I had no choice but to sink into the pleasure of the sensation.

I pulled my cock halfway out and then plunged all the way back in, a little more firmly this time. His body arched, and more moans escaped his lips. Hungry moans.

"Are you feeling alright?" I asked as I brought my lips to his.

"Yes," he managed to say. "More."

I leaned down and kissed him deeply, swirling my tongue in his mouth, taking what I wanted. I increased the pace of my movements, each thrust pushing farther inside him.

His body rocked underneath me, in perfect time with my movements. I ran my hand across his chest and down over his smooth stomach. His skin was the softest skin I had ever touched. I thought it would melt under my fingertips.

I worked my fingers back up to his nipples and gave them a gentle squeeze.

"Oh yeah," he panted, throwing his head back.

I traced my fingers along his arm to the leather restraint his wrist was in. I played with it, prodding my fingers around the edges, feeling the warmth of his flesh against the nylon material.

My balls tightened. "I'm getting close."

"I am too." He dragged his fingers through my hair and pulled it back roughly. The sting pulsed through my body as I thrust harder and harder into him.

Our orgasms hit us at exactly the same time. Our bodies convulsed in a sea of groaning, hair pulling, and swirling tongues.

I caught my breath as my body shuddered to a halt. I brushed aside a curl that had fallen onto Declan's forehead. I smiled to myself.

Going off-record had never felt this good.

CHAPTER TEN

DECLAN

I stared at the blank document on my computer as I twirled a piece of hair between my fingers. For some reason, I wasn't able to get any words out. Mel was out of the office, covering a story about a spate of armed robberies downtown, so I didn't have my cubicle neighbor to distract or inspire me.

I looked at the time in the bottom right-hand corner of the screen. I grinned at the memory of Porter jokingly chastising me to stop looking at the time at his place three nights ago.

Right, *that* was the reason I'd spent the last hour and a half staring blankly at my computer instead of actually, you know, writing the damn article I was meant to be writing.

Porter.

More specifically, sex with Porter.

The memories of that night hadn't dampened with each passing day. If anything, my constant reminiscing about what had happened between us was like lighter fluid to my soul.

I kept thinking about how good it felt to have him ask me what I wanted and then listen—really listen—to what I had said. He never questioned me or second-guessed me or...completely disregarded what I had told him and the limits I had set, the way John had. It felt right, like maybe that was the way it was meant to be.

For the first time, I was starting to think that perhaps John had been an aberration. One that had scarred me pretty badly and kept me closed off from anything that even remotely looked like BDSM.

I was so afraid of getting hurt again, both physically as well as mentally, that for such a long time, I banished any chance for a relationship, much less one that included kink, completely out of my mind.

But while the flirting in the pool had been fun, and the sex had been insanely blissful—both experiences easing the pain I was so used to living with—I had two big problems.

The first one was that while it had been off record, and I intended to completely honor that, Porter had in fact confirmed the rumors I'd heard about him from Lane and the other guys. He was a very sexually active man.

There was nothing wrong with that. I wasn't being a judgmental dick about it. I guess it just left a feeling inside of me that closely resembled being upset. Even though I had absolutely no right to be—well, anything, really.

Porter had been completely honest and upfront with me. He liked sex. He had a lot of it. He had it with me. And it really was as simple as that. I was just another notch on his bedpost—or on his under-the-bed restraints, as the case might have been.

That unpleasant burning sensation in my chest was joined by my second problem. I blinked again as I looked at the blank document in front of me. I was meant to be writing an article about the man.

I'd gone over to his place to do some informal background

research and get to know him a little bit better. I guess I had taken that to the next level.

But the issue was, I didn't really get a lot of useful information from him during the time we had spent together. Well, at least nothing fit for publication.

Which was a problem. Even though this article wasn't going to be the hard-hitting piece of investigative journalism I wanted it to be, I thought I could at least use it to illustrate my writing prowess. It didn't have to be some fluffy, dime-a-dozen puff piece, it could be something interesting. Insightful. Moving.

"Declan Davies."

I spun around in my chair to see Lane and greasy-faced Neil standing at my meager cubicle. They looked so out of place. Neil more so. He wasn't even bothering to conceal the look of disdain on his face as he looked at me and then over at my fellow cubicle colleagues.

"Oh hey, Lane. Neil," I said, sitting up a little straighter in my chair, ignoring the jolt of pain I had triggered down the left side of my back.

"We, uh, heard you're covering the Porter Jones story," Lane said, flashing me a quick smile.

"Uh, yeah," I said, standing up to cover the blank document on my screen.

"Guess your time in the big leagues was short-lived then," Neil sneered at me. I didn't know if I wanted to hit him or hand him a tissue to wipe the excess oil off his face.

"Looks like you're back to writing human interest stories. Be sure to say hi to Mrs. Langley for me when you next see her." Why was he still talking? Even Lane looked slightly uncomfortable standing beside him.

"I read your last piece by the way," Neil continued unabated. "It was brilliant. I look forward to checking that bar out. Like, *deffers*." He let out an evil cackle.

Lane elbowed him not so subtly in his side. He took a step

closer. "Look, Declan. Your mayoral exposé was really good. Not just because you got the scoop on everyone, *including us*," he turned and gave Neil an impressively shady side-eye, "but it was also really well written. You've got real talent. Make sure you use it."

And with those words of what I assumed were intended as encouragement, both men turned around and left. While they made their way back to their lofty corner offices, I turned around to face the blank screen that had filled up most of my morning, brooding over Lane's words, which were echoing in my head.

It was nice of someone like him to recognize my talent and compliment me on it. But that was the thing—it was *my talent*. They would be *my words* that I would write and publish. And it didn't feel right to try and expose Porter in the way I had exposed the mayor.

I tapped my fingers on my desk as an idea popped into my head. One that was the perfect solution. It would leave Porter untouched but give me the chance to establish my mark as a serious reporter. A total win-win.

I rubbed my hands in glee, then shut down the document I hadn't even started and jumped online. In just a few clicks, I found myself back in that same, fateful chat room, hoping that lightning could indeed strike twice.

"Oh, Porter," Mrs. Langley said to him, while she looked over at me.

Her wrinkled, but friendly, hundred-year-old face barely disguising the calculated scene that was playing out in front of me at the Daylesford Community Center.

"Thank you so much for this lovely meal you've prepared. I don't know how you do it. You're such a busy and important man, and yet you find time each week to visit us oldies and make us the most delicious, mouthwatering meals."

Porter looked down with beaming pride at the meal he had just placed on the table in front of her.

"Oh, Mrs. Langley," he said, cupping his hands in front of himself like a choirboy, "I should be the one thanking you. I really enjoy the time we get to spend together. And we have spent so much time together over the last four years, haven't we?"

If they weren't both looking at me, soooo not discreetly, I would have rolled my eyes. Instead, I forced a half-smile and nodded like an idiot. Which is what they must have thought I was, if they suspected for even a minute that I was buying this whole malarkey routine.

Every week for the last three weeks, it had been the same old thing. Different place, different people, but the scene played out like a carbon copy of the week before.

The first week, it was at the opening of Daylesford's newest library. The head librarian, Roger Simpson, made such a song and dance about how Porter was such a saint, coming down to the old library each week and taking part in reading hour for preschoolers.

Then in the second week, it was in the kitchen of a homeless shelter for which Mayor Smith's administration had—purely coincidentally, of course—recently approved funding for some much-needed renovations.

And now, here we were at the weekly 'Share A Meal, Share Your Life' initiative that Mayor Smith had come up with as a way of keeping seniors connected to people in the community by sharing a meal together, as Mrs. Langley had taken great pains to explain to me in full detail.

Three weeks, three completely stage-managed, photo-friendly opportunities.

I had to give Porter credit. He knew what he was doing, and he was doing it well. He was presenting such a positive image of himself that I began to wonder whether he had forgotten that I was a reporter for *The Daylesford Times* and not on the selection committee for the Nobel Peace Prize.

Before I could say something to excuse myself from this saccharine scene, Mrs. Langley grabbed my hand and drew me in close. I gulped. The lady was like a living national treasure. She was Daylesford's oldest and most beloved resident. In other words: someone you couldn't say no to.

"Now, dear," she said, stroking my hand gently between her soft fingers. "I know you're a very thorough reporter."

"Thank you, Mrs. Langley. I try—"

"I read your article about Mayor Smith," she interrupted as she gripped my hand with the firmness of someone sixty years younger.

"I see," I said, trying to wiggle my fingers free to no avail.

"Porter Jones is a good, proper, and upstanding man. *That's* what the people of Daylesford deserve to know."

"Of course, Mrs. Langley," I said as she released me from her iron grip.

I hid my hand behind my back, well out of her reach.

"What he does in the privacy of his bedroom is no one else's business."

My jaw fell to the floor. "I, uh...I don't know what you mean, Mrs. Langley."

"Don't you give me that *I don't know what you mean, Mrs. Langley* bullshit," she said, waving her hand dismissively in my face. "You don't get to be my age without seeing it all, young man. I have literally seen everything a human being can possibly see."

I cleared my throat, but the woman wasn't done with me yet.

"And I'll tell you one thing I know for sure, Mr. Davies."

"Yes, Mrs. Langley?" The words felt a little redundant, but I wasn't about to call her by her first name, Mary. That would have felt disrespectful.

"Life is a series of skills, behaviors, and emotions, strung together with thoughts."

"Oh, Mrs. Langley, that's so...beautiful." I was genuinely moved by her words.

Her piercing cackle filled my ears as she burst out laughing.

"That wasn't me. That was Lady Gaga," she said, her eyes twinkling mischievously.

"Here is one from me, though. The key to a good life is to simply find what makes you happy. However and in whatever way that works for you. As long as you don't hurt another person..."

I was slowly starting to compose myself.

"...Unless, of course, that's your thing."

She winked at me and let out that hearty cackle again.

And just like that, I was shocked to my very core.

Porter had wandered off during my interesting little chat with Mrs. Langley, but he returned, delicately brushing his hand against my lower back.

"Are you enjoying yourself with Declan, Mrs. Langley?" he asked as he batted his lashes in her direction.

"Oh yes, very much," Mrs. Langley replied, picking up her knife and fork and shooting me a saucy smile.

"I've enjoyed my time with Mr. Davies tremendously. And I can't wait to taste your lovely meal, Porter. I know I say it to you every week, but I am sure you have outdone yourself yet again."

We left Mrs. Langley to enjoy her meal, and once we were out of earshot, I turned to Porter and said, "Very nice. I'm very impressed. You are officially the nicest human being in the whole entire history of human beings."

Porter clutched at his chest in pretend surprise. "Who, me?" he asked, looking as sweet as pie. "Why, whatever would make you think that, Declan? I simply try to be a nice person. I'm just glad you're getting to know me better."

"I do want to get to know you better, Porter." I stepped into him so close I could smell his enticing cologne. "But I was hoping that we might be able to have another one of our off-the-record discussions."

"I see," Porter replied as he ran his fingertips over the front of my oversized, off-tangerine suit jacket. "Is that what you'd like,

Declan?" His voice was so deep and so inviting it pushed my tongue into the back of my throat, almost choking me.

"Yes," I managed to croak.

"Well, in that case," he said as a grin stretched his lips, "meet me for dinner tonight at eight."

"Sure," I breathed back, doing my best to speak with a mouth as dry as the desert.

"Oh, and Declan," he said as his light green eyes flicked up to meet mine. "Bring your appetite."

CHAPTER ELEVEN

PORTER

"Well, this is nice," I said as Declan looked around the Italian restaurant I had chosen for dinner. He had an uncertain expression on his face, but it was also the first time I was seeing him in non-business attire. And surprisingly, his normal clothes—a navy blue button-up shirt and a pair of faded black slacks—fit his lithe body well.

As I looked across the candlelit table, I realized this was the least self-conscious I had seen him. It was also the first time I had seen him in a non-professional, non-staged setting in the last three weeks.

"Are you okay?" I asked.

He took a moment to respond. "I am." He smiled. "It's, uh, been a while since we've hung out off-record."

"Yes, it has," I said, reaching for a glass of water. "I figured your editor would become suspicious if we were spending all this time together and you weren't making progress on your article."

His lips stretched out into an even wider smile and a slight blush rose to his cheeks. "Yeah, you're probably right about that."

"Are you ready to order, gentlemen?" the waiter asked as I looked down and scanned the menu. When I glanced across at Declan, the look of uncertainty from before had returned.

"If you could just give us a few minutes, please," I said. The waiter gave me a quick nod and then turned around, leaving us alone.

"Is everything alright, Declan?" I asked quietly. The restaurant was rather busy, and I didn't want anyone overhearing our conversation.

He tensed up even more. "I don't really know what to order," he said as his cheeks turned bright red. "I really only know spaghetti with meat sauce or pizza, but I'm assuming they're kind of predictable, boring choices."

I bit back my smile. "Well, we don't want to be making predictable, boring choices, now, do we?"

His face relaxed as a giggle escaped his lips.

I looked at the menu. "But if you would like something else, perhaps I could help you?"

His eyes lit up, and he nodded enthusiastically. "Yes, please."

"How hungry are you?" I asked.

"Very."

"Are you in the mood for...meat?"

Our eyes met, and a blinding heat sizzled between us. I looked back down at the menu. Right, because that's what I was doing.

"Do you like seafood?" I asked.

"I love it."

"Well then, I can recommend the seafood marinara. I've had it here a few times, and it is beautiful. Really fresh, light sauce."

"That sounds nice," Declan nodded enthusiastically. "And maybe we can get some oysters for starters? I hear they're very...."

"Gentlemen, are we ready to order?"

I looked up angrily. The waiter's timing couldn't have been worse.

We placed our orders and just as I was about to resume where we had left off, Jordan, a good-looking blond boy I had several...encounters with, walked past the table and mouthed a not very discreet "*Hi Porter*" at me.

I threw him a quick smile, and when I refocused my attention back onto Declan...I realized he had seen the whole thing. Damn it.

I hadn't been with anybody during the last three weeks, not since we'd had that night at my place. And for me, three weeks marked a very long dry spell. The funny thing was, I wasn't feeling like I was missing out on anything. I didn't seem to have the usual desire and drive for sex that I normally did.

Even though I had been doing my very best to keep things professional with Declan, or at least appearing that way to the outside world, inside, I couldn't get him out of my head.

"Who was that?" Declan asked with an arched eyebrow and a less-than-impressed tone.

"Just someone," I said vaguely. "A constituent."

"Right."

No, wait. I couldn't do it. I couldn't lie to him.

"I'm sorry, that's not entirely true," I quickly corrected myself. "He's someone that I've been with, a few times. In the past."

"That's—that's fine," Declan said, not sounding fine at all.

I didn't know what to do. This whole situation was murky at best. How was I meant to be interacting with Declan?

On the one hand, I wanted to be professional and ensure that the article he wrote about me showed me in the best possible light.

I had given up on digging around for more information because Declan wasn't giving anything away. In a way, I really respected that. It was a mark of a good reporter, protecting their sources at all costs.

But on the other hand, I couldn't get the image of Declan lying on my bed, with one cuff restraining his wrist, out of my mind.

And I didn't want to either. I wondered how much he knew about kink and whether he had any experiences with it before. I had a sense that he did, but for whatever reason, it hadn't gone so well for him.

This constant jumping back and forth between my two worlds, my professional life and my sex life, wasn't sustainable. I knew that. Declan wasn't dumb enough to be falling for all the stage-managed things I was taking him to, and it was getting harder to keep a professional relationship with him going, with the world's most serious case of blue balls happening.

Plus, it was as confusing as fuck. If I had to choose a guy to be interested in, why couldn't I have picked someone who didn't have the power to completely expose me if he knew the truth about me? That was the thing, I guess. It didn't feel like I had a choice in the matter. My feelings for Declan, whatever they were—and at this stage, I still wasn't completely sure—were completely out of my control.

"Would you like to talk about what happened between us three weeks ago?" I asked after our food had arrived and there was less chance of getting interrupted again.

"Okay," Declan said, looking at his plate. "Good call on the food, by the way. This seafood is incredible."

Those simple words made me stupidly happy for some reason. "I'm glad you're enjoying it."

Fuck it. I didn't want to keep going around and around in circles with him. I needed to put some real stuff out there...as safely as I could, of course.

"This is all strictly off-record, right?" I asked.

"It is." Declan put his fork down and stared straight at me.

"Did you enjoy what happened between us?" I asked in a hushed tone.

A lightness fell over his face, and his hazel eyes sparkled in the candlelight. "I did. I really did."

"That's good," I said. "I did, too. I guess I'm just asking because you seemed a little triggered the last time the topic moved to *non-conventional* sex."

I studied his face like a scientist peering into a microscope, searching for any signs of that same resistance that was there before. I did observe that he shuffled slightly in his seat, but it was nothing like what his previous reaction had been.

"I..." He opened and closed his mouth a few times. I could see him trying so hard to push through whatever was going on inside him, but in the end he let out a deep breath, and his shoulders slouched in defeat.

"It's okay, Declan." I reached for his hand across the table. "You don't have to tell me anything you don't want to. When the time is right, you'll know."

"Thank you." The relief in his voice was palpable.

"I guess I just don't get kink," he said after a few moments of silence.

"What about it don't you get?"

He considered my question for a few moments before responding. "Why would people who aren't in physical pain choose to do something that hurts them?"

I chewed on my food. Of course—his condition. It all made perfect sense. He must have experienced pain differently or had a different relationship to it than other people. Maybe it was a constant factor in his life, or maybe it had been something imposed on him without his say in the matter, so he wouldn't necessarily get why people would seek it out.

But his condition was another thing he wasn't ready to tell me about...yet. I was hoping that would change one day. For now, I would have to wait.

I decided to stop beating around the bush and get a little more direct with things. "I know that most people think that BDSM is all about whips, chains, and spanking, but it isn't."

Declan's expression turned curious as he tilted his head.

"I mean, hypothetically and from what I have read about it, my understanding is that it doesn't always have to be painful. Or if it is painful, the pain isn't like the bad kind of pain that we normally think of."

"It sounds like you have some experience with this, Porter."

I reached for the water and gulped it down fast. *Some experience* was putting it very mildly indeed.

"I think that there's more than one type of BDSM, just like there are so many different ways to have sex, or connect with someone, or be a Daddy."

Declan was nodding his head slowly, so I went on.

"You know...what we did at my place a few weeks ago? Well, that was a form of BDSM. And it wasn't painful, was it?"

"No," Declan responded immediately. "For the first time, I felt..." And again, he stopped himself from saying anything more.

"You can tell me, if you like." I offered a hopeful smile.

"You wouldn't understand."

"Try me."

"I can't...I'm sorry."

He bowed his head, and I felt a deep pull within me. I had to do something to earn his trust, to make him feel safe enough to be able to talk to me about these things.

If he wasn't going to tell me, then maybe I could tell him—and show him—that I knew a little more than he gave me credit for.

"I want to understand you better, Declan," I said, standing up.

"Where are you going?"

"Not far." I walked over to the empty table beside us and picked up each of the four spoons on it. Then I collected an extra two spoons from the table just slightly away from us.

As I sat back down with six spoons in my hand, he looked at me like he had absolutely no idea what was going on.

The cold metal spoons clanked in my hands as I grouped them together and placed them carefully into his hands. His expression remained frozen, looking at me as if I was borderline nuts.

"I have a friend who has chronic pain. I wanted to know what it felt like for him, so this one time, he explained it to me in the way that I'm about to explain it to you. Using spoons. Hear me out?"

I looked over at Declan expectantly and was relieved to see him nodding, agreeing to go along with this.

I tipped my head to the spoons he was holding. "For this example, we're going to assume that you have chronic pain."

"Uh, okay." Declan still looked confused, but I was hoping this would clear things up for him.

"How many spoons are you holding, Declan?"

He looked down and counted them. "Six."

"Great. So think of it like this. Each spoon represents the energy you need to do something. Like going for a walk or getting dressed in the morning, brushing your teeth, going out for lunch. Just normal, everyday things, right?"

"Sure, okay." Declan said with a small nod. His hazel eyes were still clouded with questions, but he was still going along with it. That was all I needed.

"Now, if you're a healthy person—one that doesn't experience chronic pain— you have an unlimited number of spoons at your disposal. You can just go about your day, doing everything that a healthy person can do. It doesn't cost you anything because you're able to do it automatically, almost without thinking about it. Does that make sense?"

He nodded, slightly more emphatically this time.

"But for a person who has chronic pain, they don't have an unlimited, endless supply of energy—or spoons, in this case. You only have six spoons. Think of all the things you have to do during the course of a day—from the moment you get up in the morning until you fall asleep at night—and now, try to just use the six spoons that you have to do all of those things."

His face crumpled up so cutely as he looked down at the spoons. "How do I do that?" he asked.

"Well, what's the first thing you do when you get up in the morning?"

He swallowed. "Have a shower and brush my teeth."

"Great," I said, taking one spoon away from him and placing it on my side of the table.

"And then, what do you do?"

He sucked his full lower lip in between his teeth. "Have breakfast, I guess."

"Thank you." I took another spoon.

"And then?"

"Um, then I get dressed for work."

I put another spoon over on my side of the table.

"Three spoons of energy left, Declan, and you haven't even left the house yet. Next?"

"Well, then I go to work."

"How do you get to work?"

"I walk, usually, especially if it's nice out."

"Cool, I'll take one more spoon from you, thank you."

His coffee run for his coworkers and his daily standup meeting at work brought all six spoons over to my side of the table.

"And now it's what, ten in the morning, and you're all out of energy for the day."

"Oh."

In that moment, I could see the penny dropping for Declan. He got it. He knew the point I was trying to make.

"Suddenly, normal things aren't as easy anymore, and it doesn't just affect you in not being able to do that one particular thing. It impacts your entire day, your whole life."

Declan nodded again, but this time it was a nod of pure understanding, like I was telling him something he already knew. Something that he had a lot of firsthand experience with.

"Thank you," he said as he reached for my hand across the table.

"For what?"

His eyes gave off a warm glow. "For being amazing."

I smiled, glad I had managed to communicate what I had

wanted so clearly to him. A spark of yearning simmered low in my belly as he ran his fingers across the back of my hand.

"Porter?" he asked, and I tipped my head back up to meet his gaze.

"Can we go back to your place? I have some more, uh, off-the-record things I want you to do to me."

CHAPTER TWELVE

DECLAN

The pieces of the Porter puzzle were coming together in the most unexpected of ways. And slowly, piece by piece, they were making me start to think that I could do something that I hadn't done in a very, very long time: trust someone.

It didn't take an Einstein to figure out that Porter's spoon theory conversation over dinner was his way of telling me he knew about my condition. Or at least that he had figured out that I had a condition, not necessarily the specifics of it. Having had a friend with chronic pain that seemed similar to mine meant that he at least knew a little bit about it. And yet he didn't turn and run away from me like I was some unfuckable freak.

At first, I didn't want to tell him about my scoliosis, not if I was just going to be another notch on his long line of bedpost notches. Apart from my mom, several of my closest friends, and Mel at work, it wasn't something I shared with just anyone, much less with a one-night stand. But I was starting to think that perhaps Porter could be more than just that. And even more strangely, I had a feeling that's what Porter may have wanted, too.

I might have been a little hasty in assuming Porter's professionalism over the last three weeks was a sign he wasn't interested in me. Maybe all he was doing was what we were actually meant to be doing, which was me getting information to write an article about him.

But over dinner that night—with the way he helped me choose what to order, and his gentle insistence on showing me that I was underestimating him by that whole spoon spiel he gave—those were signs that he wasn't just interested in a quick *wham, bam, thank you, Sam.* If he was, why would he be doing these sorts of things to get closer to me?

Which was a tad ironic since I was the one who was meant to be getting closer to him to know him better.

And it was also more than just a little bit scary. I hadn't let anyone in for such a long time, not since John. Even with him, I had held back. I'd had to. He had already abused the parts of me I had shared with him. If I had given all of myself to him, there would be no telling what sort of damage he would have inflicted.

It struck me that I had never truly let myself go and submitted. And yet, that was what I wanted to do more than anything else. I wanted to find a strong, dominant man that I could completely surrender to. And, more importantly, a man who understood the beauty that came with such surrender. Someone who realized that submission was a choice and one that needed to be respected at all times.

Spending time with Porter was bringing up my desire to surrender and allow another man to take control of me to the surface. And not just in the bedroom, either. I wanted someone to look after me in every way and help me make decisions in all aspects of my life.

Adulting was hard, and I clearly wasn't doing a very good job at it. I wanted someone to help me with the everyday things, so that I could focus on the really important stuff: like my career, like learning more about myself and who I really was, like experiencing the beauty that came with a complete and total transfer of power to another person.

I could see myself listening to Porter, submitting to him, and having him make decisions for me. What and when to eat, what time to go to bed, how to dress (because lord knew I needed help in that department), and all the other myriad everyday things that were clogging up my brain and making me feel like I was walking through life permanently surrounded by a heavy fog.

For me, surrender meant clarity. And I wanted to find someone that I could share that experience with, someone I could give control to, and that would help me lift the haze and become the person I was meant to be.

But finding a Daddy, a Dom who could meet my pie-in-the-sky wish list of requirements, was proving to be difficult. And with the added complication of my condition, it made the task near impossible.

But I didn't have time to be thinking about that right now. Porter and I were too busy kissing our way up the stairs toward his bedroom.

"Be careful," he said as I came perilously close to hitting the wall. He placed his hand on my lower back and gently, yet firmly, made sure I wouldn't bump into it.

"Thank you," I whispered into our kiss. I ran my fingers through his hair and pulled him hungrily toward me. That feeling of protection, of him looking out for me, unleashed a feeling of desperate desire for the man.

We reached the top of the stairs and fumbled our way into the bedroom and, finally, onto the bed. He was gentle with me all the way, treating me as if I were made from porcelain. Knowing that he was doing it deliberately, as a sign of respect for the limitations of my body, turned me on like crazy. I loved feeling so safe with him.

The only slightly strange thing he was doing was that he was nibbling on my lower lip a lot more. It was like he had just discovered it, and it was his favorite thing ever. Not that I was complaining one bit.

"God, I love your lower lip," he said, managing to tear himself away from it.

Ha, I knew it. That would help explain why he had been focused in on it—chewing, nibbling, and licking it with such unbridled abandon.

It was my turn to return the compliment. "Yeah, well, I love your goofy smile."

His brows furrowed. "What do you mean, my *goofy smile?*"

I pulled away slightly. His eyes had narrowed, and his face grew serious and very un-goofy.

"You know, the one where your eyes go all googly and uneven."

I was met by even more seriousness crossing his face.

"It doesn't happen all the time," I explained. "Only when you smile and really mean it. And it's so freaking adorably cute."

His face softened a little as he mulled my words over. "You don't know you have the most adorable smile ever?" I asked.

"Clearly not." And with that, his face broke out into *that look* that I just loved so much.

"So," he said, dragging his eyes up and down my body. "What would you like to do tonight, Declan? Same as last time?"

"No." I inhaled sharply. "More. Tie up both hands, please. I'm ready to move on to intermediate level."

His eyes lit up with excitement at my words, but then he brought himself back down to reality. "Oh, baby, don't rush this. Let's stick to beginner level for a while longer and enjoy the journey. Believe me, every single step of it will be fun."

I sank further into the bed and further into the excitement those words elicited in me. Sure, I could take it slow with this man. And he was right, in a way: that's exactly what I needed.

He walked around the bed and this time lifted up the wrist restraints from underneath each side.

"Same safeword?" he asked, standing just off to my side.

I looked up and practically inhaled the man with my eyes. "McBeal, yes," I said as I felt his fingers tracing the ridge across my shoulder.

Normally, I buckled at touch, any touch. It was an involuntary reaction, as if my body would go into a brace position, not wanting to get hurt or feel pain.

But not with him. He calmed me down, soothed my body. His fingers felt divine as they grazed over my shirt. If anything, he left me wanting more. I wanted his fingers under my shirt and pressing into my skin. Going wherever they wanted to go, taking whatever they wanted to take.

The feeling of wanting him to take me overpowered me, and I pressed myself into his touch. He knelt on the bed as his arms wrapped around my back, slowly and with such control that I felt my body melting into the surrender. A soft moan escaped my lips and he kissed into it. I felt his teeth nibbling on my lower lip.

He kept on kissing me while his skilled fingers effortlessly removed my shirt. He pulled away and made his way down to my feet, taking off my shoes and socks with care. Next, he unbuckled my pants, pulling them down my legs and lifting me up slowly to completely remove them.

I was lying on his bed, naked except for my briefs, which were doing a pitiful job of hiding my hard-on. Porter took me in like he had reached the peak of the mountaintop and was admiring the view.

"Do you have any idea how beautiful you are, Declan?" His tone was low, deep, and hit me right in the chest.

I felt my skin flush with warmth. I was completely exposed in front of him, yet I felt so safe and protected.

"I mean it," he continued as he grazed his fingertips over my lower abdomen and up toward my chest. "Every single part of you is so spectacular. Your wavy hair, your soulful eyes, your sweet and juicy lower lip, and your body..."

My breath hitched in my throat. I hated my body. It didn't look right. It didn't feel right. I was constantly in some kind of pain or experiencing a limitation, something I couldn't do.

He ran his eyes up and down the entire length of me, before turning his gaze to meet me straight on.

"Your body makes me want to do things that I've never even thought of doing."

"What? Like tying me up?" I cringed at the stupidity of my joke.

"No," Porter said, remaining serious and thankfully ignoring my misfired attempt at humor.

"Like protect you." His fingers reached my pecs and traced gentle circles around my sensitive nipples.

"Like cherish you." He leaned down and brought his lips to my nipples, gently lapping at them.

"Like devour you." And with that, his mouth lunged at my throat and bit around my Adam's apple. I stretched my head back, giving him all the access he needed.

He kept nibbling at my throat while his hands stretched down the length of my arms. He stopped chewing at my neck only to place my wrists into the restraints.

"Are you comfortable, Declan?" His light green eyes were filled with seriousness as he looked at me intently.

"Yes, I am. Thank you."

His fingers traced my jawline. "If that ever changes, if you ever want to stop for any reason, use the safeword. Okay?"

I gave a quick, slightly impatient nod. "I will."

"I will be so proud of you if you do. I want you to know that."

And with that, he pulled down my briefs and grabbed my cock in his warm fingers. He formed a tight fist as he worked up and down the length of my shaft.

That sensation felt incredible, but it didn't even come close to what I was feeling by being tied up.

I had a love/hate relationship with my body, and ninety-nine percent of the time, I hated it. The constant pain and the increasing curvature in my spine were constant reminders I could never escape from. They were always there, something I either felt in my body or saw in myself.

But the moment Porter slipped my wrists into the nylon restraints, it was like everything changed. Suddenly, there was a new feeling inside of me. It might have only been one percent of love in the whole love/hate equation, but it was strong enough to push everything else away.

As I lay on the bed, restrained, watching Porter put a condom on and lube himself up, tenderly applying some onto my hole as well, my body ached not with pain, but with excitement. With freshness, a hungry need, and a hope that with it, for at least a while, I would be transported to a place where the pain I normally felt didn't exist.

I felt one of Porter's lubed up fingers gently tapping the sensitive skin around my entrance. It felt raw and enticing and I couldn't wait for more.

His finger entered me as a soft moan escaped my lips. He began sliding in and out of me, loosening me up to get me ready. He added another finger, then another, both slicked with lube, stretching me even wider.

"Are you ready?" Porter asked as he gently spread my ass with his lubed-up fingers.

"Yes, I am." I looked him straight in the eyes as he lifted my legs and placed them against his broad, tanned shoulders.

I closed my eyes and let out a deep breath as he entered me in one steady movement. A feeling of fullness washed over me as I surrendered my body to him. He thrust into me, slowly at first, and gradually building up momentum. With one hand, he tweaked my nipple, gently pinching it. I let out a low hiss at the intensity of the pleasure it produced.

His other hand wrapped firmly around the base of my cock and he began stroking me. "I'm close," I warned him.

"Good," he replied with a twinkle in his eye. "I want you to come."

He sped up his rhythm, both with his hips and with his hands. My body was overloading on all the incredible feelings I was experiencing. My wrists tied up, my hole pounded by his cock, his fingers wrapped around my dick, jerking furiously. Urgently. Powerfully.

After just a few more strokes, I reached the edge, crying out and twisting as my orgasm exploded. Porter kept stroking until I was completely and utterly spent. A few seconds later, I could feel his cock releasing inside of me, his body bucking wildly as he came hard.

He stayed inside of me, his cock still semi-hard. His body kept shuddering sporadically, as if he were experiencing the aftershocks of his orgasm.

He brought his fingers to my mouth. I looked at them—they were covered with my cum.

"Lick them." It was a command, not a question.

I had never tasted myself before and was caught a little off guard. The thought of using the safeword was a fleeting one because I wanted to try this. I wanted to do this. For him.

He placed his fingers just in front of my lips. I looked up at him as I licked his fingers completely clean. When I was done, his mouth crashed into mine, our tongues swirling around, sharing the saltiness between our mouths.

He was still inside of me. "Don't pull out," I managed to say.

"I have no intention to," he whispered back.

And we lay there, kissing my cum between us, with me tied up and him inside me, for the most blissful few moments of my life.

"So," I finally said once we had swallowed all of my release. "This is still beginner level, right?"

He smiled at me adorably. "It is, my beautiful boy. This is only the beginning."

CHAPTER THIRTEEN

PORTER

The email notification on my phone let out a loud ping as I drove into the parking lot at Deffers. I found an empty spot, pulled into it, and reached for my phone.

My chest tightened. It was an email from the mayor.

I may or may not have been trying to avoid him for the past several days. I knew full well what he was chasing, but I didn't really have any updates for him. Well, none that I could share with him.

I leaned back and smiled as thoughts of Declan lying tied up on my bed came flooding back to me. The way he looked at me was a heady mixture of innocence and hunger. The way his body responded to mine was pure dynamite. The way he lapped up his cum off my fingers...well, it was getting me hard thinking about it days later.

Declan ignited an instinct in me that I'd never felt before. Normally, my desire was all about sex, and for all of my life, I thought that's all there was. Sex. Bodies. Positions. Moves. It was almost a little mechanical—fun as all fuck, but a process. A series of steps that led to a predictable, mutually agreed upon result.

And then it was over with that guy—or guys—and it would be onto the next wild adventure. The momentum of arousal and curiosity seemed never-ending, like it would continue forever.

But with Declan, the desire for the next shiny new thing came to a complete stop. A dead end. Even if I had wanted to, I couldn't muster up that same level of desire within me for anything else, for anyone else, but him.

He was not only enough, he was more than anything I could have imagined in even my kinkiest dreams. And the best bit? We were still only at beginner level.

And we hadn't even come close to discussing the one thing that I really wanted, one of the few things that I hadn't actually ever done with anyone else: A contract. But that would have to wait. I wasn't ready to go there, yet.

I fought back my smile as I returned my gaze to the email and read it. To my surprise, the mayor was actually happy with what I was doing or—at least, what he thought I was doing. Because even though I hadn't really been focused on it as much as I should have been, no more embarrassing stories had come out about the mayor, and certainly nothing pegging-related. I breathed a sigh of relief.

Even more importantly than that, the selfie scandal was actually starting to die down on its own. Nothing new had been added to the fire, so it was simply running out of steam. The media was looking to move on to the next story, the next scandal, and I was perfectly happy to let them.

We had also successfully managed to avoid the biggest calamity of all, quashing resignation rumors quickly and ferociously whenever they flared up, not allowing them to get any traction or inflict any serious damage on the mayor.

So, maybe I had done a better job than I gave myself credit for. I got out of the car and walked into the bar, reflecting on how strange it was that I wasn't as hyper-focused on my work as I normally was. I guess I had other things on my mind.

It was mid-afternoon, so the bar wasn't that busy. Steel, Stirling, and I had decided to meet up for a cheeky little catch-up. It had been a while since just us Daddies had some time together, and as much as I liked Mikey and Nick, I did miss spending time with just my closest friends.

I joined the two men perched at the end of the bar, greeting them warmly with a hug.

"It's so good to see you both," I said as I sat down.

"The usual, Porter?" Steel asked as he lifted his hand in the air to get the bartender's attention.

"Sure, why not? It's not like I'm going back to the office after this."

"You're not?" Stirling asked, shooting me a baffled look as Steel ordered us a round of drinks.

I shook my head. "No, I'm, uh...catching up with Declan."

Two sets of eyes narrowed in on me as I adjusted my shoulders under the weight of their glares.

"The reporter?" Stirling asked.

"The reporter who exposed the mayor?" Steel added.

"Yeah, that's the one," I said as I grabbed the drinks the bartender had brought over. "Cheers," I said, not waiting for the others to raise their glasses and taking a sip of the vodka soda. I hadn't spoken to the guys about Declan, yet, but I needed to. I wanted to get their perspective on things.

"Sounds like something is going on here, Porter," Steel observed. I looked over at the guys and was met with two friendly, familiar, expectant faces.

It was funny. Over the years, I had told them pretty much everything, down to the most explicit and intimate details of my sex life. They were my only outlet, the only people in the world I could share that part of my life with.

And yeah, maybe I overshared, just slightly. But I was backed into a corner in every other aspect of my life. I didn't have any other option, really. They were the only people I could be my true self with, the only people I didn't have to suppress who I was and put on an act for.

So why was I suddenly finding it hard to tell them about Declan? It didn't make any sense.

"Hey, do you guys think I have a goofy smile?"

"Huh?" both men said in almost perfect unison.

"I can't say I've ever really noticed," Stirling said.

"Yeah, me either," Steel chipped in.

"How can you guys not notice?" I asked, slightly irritated.

"I don't know," Steel shot back. "I guess I just don't look at you that way, Porter. You're like the annoying little brother I'm glad I never had."

Stirling let out a laugh until I shot him an evil look.

I sighed.

I guess that was the beauty of having friends that you had known for so long. There were things about them that you just didn't notice because you were just so used to them. And the really great thing was that even though they were both attractive men in their own right, none of us had ever blurred the boundaries of friendship by sleeping with each other.

Yep, not even me, the Samantha of the group. I drew a line at that. Besides, it would have felt weird and wrong on so many levels. They weren't just my friends, they were more like brothers.

Brothers who clearly didn't notice whether I had an unusual smile or not.

"Why do you want to know about your smile all of a sudden?" Stirling asked.

"No reason," I said, trying to brush it off. It didn't make the slightest bit of sense, but I wasn't ready to talk about Declan for some reason. Not even with these guys.

"How are things with you and Nick going?" I asked Steel, eager to change the topic.

"Well," Steel began, clearing his throat. "I actually need your advice on this one. Especially yours, Porter, given that you're so...experienced."

I breathed a sigh of relief into my drink, happy that the conversation had successfully moved on.

"Sure, hit me up," I said, flashing them a wide smile. They did both look a little longer at me than normal, as if they were looking to see something new in my face. "What seems to be the problem?"

Steel scratched the back of his head. "Well, you both know we're trying out this whole age play thing, right?"

Stirling and I nodded.

"And to tell you the truth, it's not exactly going smoothly."

It was times like these that I really missed having Hudson here. He was great for conversations like this, being able to balance being respectful and supportive and yet somehow managing to get just the right amount of information out of you at the same time too.

"What do you mean by that? How are things not going smoothly?" I asked, channeling my inner Hudson.

Steel shot me a slightly funny look, but then he considered my question. "Nick is not a typical boy, like, say, Mikey is."

Stirling's face lit up at the mention of his boy. "But Mikey is one in a million."

"Oh, of course," Steel said, nodding emphatically. "I didn't mean it like that at all. I just meant that Mikey is a good boy, whereas Nick is, well, let's just say he's a handful."

"All good." Stirling gave Steel a friendly clap on his back. "I know exactly what you mean, and I don't envy you at all."

We all let out a low chuckle.

"Nick is unique and unbelievable and brilliant, but he's never had any experience with being a little. And my only experience with age play has been with boys who were established. They knew what they liked, what they wanted, and how to go about it. That made it easier for me as their Daddy to interact with them. With Nick, I actually feel really lost and...inadequate."

"Hey, it's okay to feel a little unsure of yourself whenever you try something new, Steel." I looked over at Stirling, who was nodding in agreement.

I continued. "This is something that you and Nick can explore together. If you want to make it work, the solution really is simple. Right, Stirling?"

He let out a hearty laugh, remembering my patented three-point plan of love that helped bring him and Mikey together. "Yes, take it from me, Steel," Stirling chimed in. "Just talk to him. Tell him how you're feeling and what you're going through. Get him to do the same, and then at least you're on the same page."

I could see Steel processing what we were saying to him. Stirling's words echoed in my mind, too. What page were Declan and I on? Was it the same one? I had no idea what he wanted out of this thing between us, if he even wanted anything at all.

But before we talked about that, there was one thing the mayor had asked me in his email to find out. I had given up on trying to get Declan to reveal his source to me, and fair enough, reporters guarded that secret with their lives. But the mayor did want me to make sure that there was nothing else that Declan knew about him...especially his proclivities for getting pegged by Peggy.

Declan and I had agreed to meet the next day for after-work drinks. I'd chosen a relaxed but upscale bar, a few blocks away from *The Daylesford Times* office. I was hoping the proximity to his work would help me keep the conversation focused on what I needed it to be: Work. With maybe a little pleasure thrown in on the side.

I saw him as soon as he walked in, dressed as always in a hideous suit that was clearly designed by someone who hated humanity, and looking like he was puffing and out of breath. He was only a few minutes late, but maybe he had run over. I waved, and when he saw me, a smile spread across his face. He gave a quick wave back as he made his way over to me.

"Hey, Declan," I said, eyeing him up and down, but seeing the image of him naked and tied to my bed, not the off-peach polyester monstrosity he was trapped in.

"Hey, Porter. Sorry I'm late. I got caught up on something."

"It's okay," I said, motioning for him to sit down across the small corner table I was seated at. "I hope you didn't run over here."

A look of guilt washed over his face. "I did, yeah." His tone was sheepish. "I didn't want to be late and make you..."

"Here, I ordered you a lemonade. Have some." He sipped it gratefully through the straw as I studied him. His forehead was beaded with sweat, he was sitting awkwardly in the seat, and he just looked all sorts of dishevelled and uncomfortable.

Why was he so worried about being a few minutes late? Something had definitely happened to him to make him like this. Something...or someone. I wanted to find out so desperately, but I had to fight those feelings away.

No, this had to be a business talk. Hopefully we could talk about other things later. Preferably with a whole lot less clothes on.

Declan slurped up the last of the lemonade noisily. "Better?" I asked.

His cheeks flushed slightly as he nodded and settled back into the chair. I'd never know how he was able to crack through all of my walls and make me want to look out for him, but somehow, he was able to do it.

I cleared my throat. "We need to talk. About work."

"Sure," he said with a smile. "Is this an off-the-record chat?"

"Technically, yes," I said, returning his smile. "But it's not *that* kind of off-the-record conversation."

"Well, what kind is it then?"

I secretly loved it when he got a little cocky and full of himself. Much like his work outfits, it totally didn't suit him, and he wasn't able to pull it off at all. I just liked the fact that he was trying. It was cute, even though that was probably the last thing he was going for. I had no intention of breaking that bubble for him.

"Look, Declan, I don't expect you to reveal the source of your information to me."

He sat up a little straighter. "Good. Because I have no intention of telling you."

"Fair enough," I conceded. "But I would like to ask you another question. I think it is one that you should be able to answer."

"And what might that be?" His lips were pressed tight, but his eyes remained warm.

"I need to know if you have anything else on the mayor. Any dirt on him that could potentially hurt him in what is, as you well know, an election year."

There, I'd said it. It was a question I would have asked any other reporter in the city, and given how well I got on with most of them, I would have expected an honest answer in return.

Declan wasn't just any other reporter, though. So I guess from him, I definitely expected an answer, and I sure as hell wasn't expecting him to be as evasive as he was.

"I can't tell you that, Porter."

My mouth gaped open in surprise. "And why not?"

"Because it would be unprofessional of me. We both have our jobs to do. You know that. I don't stick my nose into your work, so why are you sticking yours into mine?"

I certainly wasn't expecting that level of fiery defiance from him. It bothered me. I wasn't trying to do anything underhanded or anything I wouldn't have expected from any other reporter, so why was he being like this?

"Hey, Porter. Good to see you." I looked up and saw a boy I had met on Gruff and hooked up with a few times, Jeremy, standing in front of us. He was blond, tall, and well built. Definitely a boy, but more of a twunk than a twink.

"Uh, hi, Jeremy," I said. As I looked over, I could see Declan bristling, his eyes shooting daggers at Jeremy—and me.

Jeremy looked over at Declan and smiled awkwardly. "I don't mean to interrupt," he said, totally interrupting, "just thought I would come over and say hello. That's all."

"And you've said it."

Jeremy and I turned our heads to Declan, and a small part of me was pleased at the snarkiness Jeremy's presence brought out in him.

"Well, I'll be off then. Maybe I'll see you sometime, Porter?"

And with that, he flashed me a quick smile, deliberately avoided even looking in Declan's direction, and left.

"Another constituent?" Declan snapped, not even waiting for Jeremy to be properly out of earshot.

"No, a boy I've played with a few times," I mumbled.

This conversation was proving to be challenging enough without having to bring in my own sexual history into the mix as well. We were meant to be talking business after all, and I was still slightly pissed at Declan for his response to my question.

"I'd be surprised if he even knew how to vote." Declan's eyes were fixated on Jeremy, and he only seemed to relax slightly once Jeremy had left the bar entirely.

"Am I picking up on some jealousy here?" I said, half-teasingly.

"No, you are not." Declan's entire demeanor had changed. He was stiff and had a cold edge to him. "And you cannot just use me, and the fact that we have had sex as a way to get me to do what you want."

"Declan, that's not what I'm doing at all," I protested. It really wasn't, and I hated that he had that misconception about what was happening.

"I genuinely like you," I continued. "Look, let's get outta here and go back to my place? We can talk about it some more there."

"I can't," he said as he stood up.

Wait, he was leaving already? What was going on here?

"I've got dinner with my mom tonight," he offered by way of explanation. "Was there anything else, Porter?"

The way he said my name sent a cold shiver through me. It was so...clinical.

"Uh, yeah, just one more thing. I can't make our appointment tomorrow." Declan was meant to be following me around in the afternoon for the story. "Something's come up."

"That's fine. We can reschedule."

"Okay, great. Well, that's it, then."

And with that, I watched as Declan forced a smile and walked away from me and out of the bar. I followed him until his off-peach suit disappeared completely out of view.

What the fuck had just happened?

CHAPTER FOURTEEN

DECLAN

I was still fuming at Porter in the Uber ride from the bar to my mom's place. The thing was, I didn't know why, exactly.

It's not like Porter had done anything wrong. He just wanted to talk about the article, which he was perfectly entitled to do. After all, it was the reason why we were even spending any time together in the first place.

But as I looked out at the streets of downtown Daylesford from the backseat of the car, a gnawing feeling made its way up my chest before settling in my throat. The words were there. They were close. I just couldn't articulate them.

Was I worried that Porter was only using me to make sure I didn't write any more damaging stories about the mayor? I had thought that at first, but the more time we spent together, and especially after dinner and sex at his place last week, I didn't think that anymore. Even the conversation we'd just had at the bar, while it bubbled that fear up to the surface, I knew it wasn't what had gotten me so off balance.

No, something else was bothering me. Ever since I'd received an email that morning, a seed of guilt had been planted. And Porter's conversation, and his wanting to know if I had any more dirt on the mayor, ripped right into the heart of that guilty feeling.

Because the fact of the matter was that I *did* have more dirt on the mayor. And if Porter thought the selfie sexting story was bad, what I had just learned was going to be ten times worse.

I felt trapped. This wasn't what I had wanted. When I had reached out to time2telldatruth again, it wasn't to get more dirt on the mayor. It was, in the interest of balance, to get something on his opponent. That was my brilliant, win-win plan. Or so I thought. I still managed to get my hard-hitting story, but it wouldn't affect Porter. And it wouldn't affect *us*.

As it turned out, though, the opposition leader Leigh Mathison was totally clean. So clean that even the seedy underbelly of the internet, the dark web, couldn't bring up anything even remotely controversial about the man. There was literally nothing new I could find on him that wasn't already known or in the public domain.

Whereas with Mayor Smith, there was something. Time2telldatruth had said it was super hard to find, but he did. And it was a doozy of a bombshell.

I thanked the driver and got out, making my way up the front path of Mom's tiny house on the outskirts of Daylesford. It was run-down and in need of massive renovations, but after so many years of scrimping and saving, it was all she could afford. At least it was her own place. She was proud of it, and so was I. It was a testament to all of her willpower, dedication, and damn hard work.

"Declan." She beamed as she opened the creaky front door to let me in. "How are you, baby?"

"I'm good, Mom. I'm good," I said, sinking into her soft hug, gently blowing away a strand of her shoulder-length brown hair that had made its way to my mouth. But I wasn't good, far from it. I was torn in a way I knew that only she would understand.

"Honey, what is it?" she asked, scanning my face worriedly. We had the same hazel eyes, and sometimes it felt like I was looking in the mirror when I looked into them.

She was a truly beautiful woman. Friendly eyes, a wide, inviting smile, and the most open and forgiving personality I had ever come upon. Despite all the reasons she had to be bitter and twisted about the shit life had thrown her way, she was the exact opposite of all of that. She was compassionate, caring, and committed to always doing the right thing.

I followed her into the small living area, and we both sat down on the couch we'd had for as long as I could remember. It was a faded navy color, but it was as familiar as it was comfortable.

"Dinner's still a while off, but you look like you could use a drink." She smiled as she said it.

"No, I'm okay, Mom. But I do need to talk."

Her face turned serious again. "What is it, Declan? Has something happened at work?"

"Yeah, you could say that."

I proceeded to tell her the whole story about Porter. Well, maybe not the whole story. I left out anything that involved getting tied up.

"So, it sounds like you're developing feelings for this man," she observed and, as always, hit the nail on the head.

Mom was good like that. We were close, and I could tell her anything. For a moment, my thoughts turned to Porter and how his parents had thrown him out when they had discovered he was gay.

I never had that issue with my mom. From the moment I came out to her when I was fourteen, she was my number one supporter. It was never a big deal or some terrible problem we had to overcome.

I guessed she knew a thing or two about being ostracized herself, and she never wanted me to have to experience anything like that. Being a single mother wasn't exactly what her parents had wanted for her, and while they might not have thrown her out of their home, it did strain relations with them for a very long time. I had very few memories of my grandparents growing up.

"I have more information about the mayor," I said, falling back into the comfortable familiarity of the leather couch.

"Right," Mom said as her hazel eyes filled up with a look of understanding. "So, on the one hand, you have a major story that you could report on which would be great for you professionally."

"Uh-huh."

"But on the other hand, it would be bad for you on a personal level. If you go ahead with the story, this man that you are developing feelings for will get hurt."

"Exactly." I let out a desperate sigh. "And he won't just be hurt, Mom—he will hate me and never want to speak to me again."

"Oh, baby." She placed her soft hand around my fingers and gave me a warm smile. "It's a tough situation you're in."

"What should I do, Mom? I mean, you have every reason to hate Mayor Smith. Why aren't you just telling me to go ahead with it and publish the damn story and ruin his career?"

"Honey, I don't hate that man. Life's too short for that." She looked around the room, collecting her thoughts. "Focus on what you want and on what's right. Be clear on that. I mean, really clear on that in your own mind, Declan. That will be your anchor as you navigate the choppy waters of whatever you decide to do."

"But what about Porter?" I asked with a desperate, almost pleading tone in my voice. "If I go ahead and publish this story about Mayor Smith, it will make things impossible between Porter and me. There's no way that whatever is happening between us will be able to continue."

"Baby," Mom said as she gave my hand a squeeze, "if something is meant to happen between you and Porter, then it will. Sure, he'll be upset for a while. But remember why you did it. Keep coming back to it. That will be your anchor, remember?"

I let out another sigh. I still didn't know what to do next, but Mom's words definitely made sense.

I had a sinking feeling that whatever happened, whatever choice I made about whether to run the story or not, I'd be needing to cling to that anchor like my life depended on it.

The next day, I was returning to the office after covering a story about a suburban house fire. Thankfully, no one had been hurt, and the damage to the property was minimal, as well. It was one of those filler stories that the paper covered. A story that I was getting increasingly frustrated that I was still being forced to cover.

I was sitting on the biggest political scandal in Daylesford's history, and yet that was exactly it. I was sitting on it. Waiting. For what, I didn't know. Some sign or divine intervention to guide me down the right path.

I had been scheduled to hang out with Porter for the afternoon, but after he cancelled, I had some free time, so I was in no rush to return to the office. My thoughts were all over the place anyway, so I decided to drive around downtown aimlessly for a while, letting my thoughts drift in and out.

After about ten minutes, I was stopped at a red light when I turned my gaze and saw Porter on the sidewalk. He was pushing a man in a wheelchair. I blinked a few times, as if to confirm that it really was him. He'd said he had another appointment that afternoon, but he never said what that appointment was. Or who it was with.

What was going on?

The light turned green, but I managed to pull over into an empty parking spot. I got out of my car and followed Porter and the man he was with, suddenly feeling like I was a spy in a James Bond movie. I couldn't walk too quickly because everytime I did, my back seized up on me. It had been playing up since the moment I had gotten out of bed.

I managed to keep a good amount of distance—and people—between us. The last thing I needed was for Porter to turn around and catch me stalking him like some, well, stalker. I may have embarrassed myself a few times in front of the man, but that would have been an all-time low, even for me.

Why was I even doing this? Why was I interested in what Porter was doing? There was a curiosity that was driving me, a curiosity that I didn't fully understand.

After walking down a few more blocks, Porter suddenly turned his head and began looking around. I quickly managed to duck behind a light pole to hide myself from his view, silently thanking myself for wearing a gray suit that day.

After a few moments, I peeked around and saw Porter and the man walking into a place. I looked up at the sign and had to swallow hard to alleviate some of the tightness that had formed at the base of my throat.

Porter and the man had stepped into Revolver.

I was frozen, glued to the light pole. I didn't know what to do next. That's where it had happened. That was the place of both my greatest shame and my biggest realization.

John was a member of Revolver and had been for a number of years before we had met. He knew a lot of the people there, but I got the distinct impression that he wasn't necessarily liked by many of them. He was always a little aloof, preferring to keep everyone at arm's length.

We went there maybe about a dozen times during our relationship. And every time we did, I couldn't help but notice how the other Daddies and Doms treated their boys. They all shared a lot of common characteristics: the Daddies and Doms were strong, decisive, decision-makers. That part made sense to me.

But then there was a flipside to their interactions that I observed as well. There was tenderness, caring, listening. All things that felt so alien to me because they were none of the things that I experienced with John.

One day, John and I were in the middle of a scene where he had tied me up. That day, my back was really playing up bad, and I was in a fair bit of pain. I let John talk me into going anyway, and against my better judgment, I listened to him and not the signals my body was giving me.

The scene started off slow and gentle. He tied up my feet first, and when he got to my left wrist, that's when it happened. A searing bolt of pain tore through the entire right side of my back, shoulder, and up into my neck.

I asked him to stop. I used the safeword.

Loudly.

Clearly.

Repeatedly.

And as always, he ignored me.

Luckily for me, there were people watching the scene who stepped in. I didn't remember much of what happened next. My subconscious must have tried to push it down as far as it would go. But I knew it got ugly.

People were yelling. John was arguing. I even vaguely remember John throwing a punch at someone. Needless to say, his membership got revoked, and we never went back there again.

We broke up shortly after that. In a way, that awful experience was the lightbulb moment I needed to have. For some reason, when he mistreated me in the privacy of our own home, it felt less bad, somehow. I knew what was happening wasn't right, but part of me did question whether I was doing something wrong.

With the scene at Revolver though, and seeing other people's strong reactions to his behavior, it cemented in me that what he was doing was so way over the line that there was no coming back from it. We fought bitterly for weeks after that scene, and I moved out shortly after.

I hadn't been back to Revolver since. And now Porter had just walked in there with some guy. Great, this was just what I needed. As if my mind wasn't cloudy enough, now *this* had happened.

I stepped away from the light pole and brushed off the arm of my suit. I slowly made my way back to my car.

I still had no clue whether I should write the article about Mayor Smith.

I was torn about my feelings for Porter and where we were at.

And I was confused as fuck at the sight of him stepping into Revolver with another man.

What the hell was I going to do about any of it?

CHAPTER FIFTEEN

PORTER

The mayor barged into my office, slamming the door behind him. He threw a cell phone onto my desk. I looked up at him, confused. His face was fiery red, and his nostrils were beyond flaring.

"What's going on?" I picked up the cell phone and looked at it. My eyes filled with horror at the lead story.

Mayor and Wife Peggy, Caught in the Act.

The pegging story was out—and accompanied by a series of grainy photos.

I dropped the phone when I saw the byline.

Declan Davies.

How could he have done this in the first place, much less without even giving me fair warning? My blood started boiling, but I didn't have time to entertain my own feelings. Mayor Smith was pacing furiously up and down my office.

"William, I had no idea..."

He shot me a look that I thought would literally kill me. "That's exactly it. You have no fucking idea, Porter. You were meant to handle this. I thought you were on top of it."

"I was—I mean, I am, handling it."

"Well, clearly not well enough."

The mayor stopped pacing and just looked at me, his eyes filled with a dark storm of rage, shame, and sorrow.

We both knew it as we stared at each other in shocked silence. He was done. There was no coming back from this. The damage was too deep. Even though it was a private act between two consenting adults, society wasn't ready, and even Daylesford wasn't ready to accept something like this.

The pain clenched my chest so hard that it hurt. "William, I am so truly sorry..."

"Save it, Porter. I'm ruined. My career. My reputation. And...Peggy." His voice broke as he said his wife's name, bringing his knuckle to his mouth. "The shame of this is... Our families... How are we ever supposed to...?"

His voice trailed off, but I didn't say anything. There was nothing I could say, and he wouldn't have been interested in anything coming from me at this point anyway.

I knew he wouldn't have believed me, but my heart broke for him and Peggy. I couldn't even imagine what she was going through.

"Can you get Warren to prepare my resignation statement?"

"Of course," I said around the lump that had formed in my throat. "Is there anything else I can do?"

He looked like he wanted to fire back with something toxic and mean, but after a few moments, a dejected look fell across his face. His shoulders slumped as he picked up the cell phone from my desk and walked over to the door.

"Congratulations, Porter," he said as he turned to face me. "The deputy mayor will take over until the election, but I know he won't contest it. So it looks like you've got a clear path to get what you always wanted."

He opened the door and walked out, closing it gently behind him.

I fell back into my chair, completely stunned.

He was right. This was what I had always wanted. The top job in the city. But not like this. Never in my wildest dreams had I thought this was the way things would play out.

And it was all because of one person. My jaw clenched as a red-hot fury rose in my chest. I grabbed my car keys and stormed out of the office, headed to see the person who had inflicted all of this damage.

He'd ruined not just one politician's career, but two people's lives.

Well, three if I included myself in that list. How could he not have given me a heads up about this? He had to have known how nuclear-level-damaging this would be. And yet—nothing. He didn't say a word beforehand.

I expected that kind of behavior from an enemy, not from... well, whatever I thought Declan was to me.

I was going to find out what the hell was going through his mind and why he hadn't told me what he was planning to do.

CHAPTER SIXTEEN

DECLAN

Mel and I stared at each other in disbelief. I turned back to face the screen and blinked several times.

One hundred thousand views.

That was how many clicks my story had generated in just three hours since it was released, not just smashing, but annihilating, the previous record.

"This is amazing." Her cherry-pink lips stretched out in a wide smile as she delicately placed her hand on my forearm. "You've broken the biggest story in *The Daylesfords Times*' history. You should be so thrilled about this, Declan."

She was right. I should have been, but I wasn't. Not even for a second, because I knew what the consequences would be. Porter Jones would hate me and, most likely, never speak to me again. Well, after he yelled and screamed at me, I assumed. I had that to look forward to, as well.

The thought of him being furious at me killed me, but what was

I supposed to do? If I passed on the story, somebody else would have picked it up and ran with it.

And yeah, there were a lot of dubious ethical elements to the story which I wasn't proud of. But this got my foot well and truly in the door. It would be the first—and last—time that I would ever do anything like this.

Maybe I could make Porter believe it too. And hey, in some ways, this could even be a good thing for him. I'd heard rumors that he was eyeing the mayor's position. This could be his opening, paving the way for his ascension. Maybe he'd even be happy, thankful.

Oh, who was I kidding? That was just wishful-borderline-deranged thinking. I was well and truly screwed.

"Mr. Jones, you can't go in there. Mr. Jones, please!" I heard our receptionist Monica's voice ring out.

Mel twisted around, and her eyes widened in disbelief. "Holy shit. Declan, he's here."

"Who?" I asked as I turned around, my brain clearly not keeping up with what I was hearing.

And there he was. One raging, fuming, firestorm of a man approaching my cubicle, getting angrier with every step he took as he marched closer to me. I swallowed and looked around my cubicle helplessly, as if there was some secret trap door or magical escape chute I could propel myself into.

Porter reached my cubicle, with Monica following close behind. "Mr. Jones, you really can't be here—"

He raised his hand in the air, silencing her.

I stood up. It felt almost surreal to be standing so close to him with him looking the way he was at me. It was a universe apart from the way he had looked at me when I was tied up on his bed. For a moment, I felt dizzy, disoriented.

"Porter, what are you doing? You have no right to be here."

"I have every right to be here." His words rang out across the entire floor, which suddenly fell into a hushed silence. He and I both looked around. Everyone's eyes were on us. I became acutely aware of the scene his presence, and his volume, was creating.

"Mr. Jones, if you don't leave now, I will call security," Monica insisted.

"It's okay, Monica," I said, shooting her a reassuring, and at the same time apologetic, smile. "I will meet with Mr. Jones in a private meeting room and let everyone else get back to their work." That seemed to snap everyone out of their stunned silence, and people went back to whatever they were doing as Porter followed me into the boardroom.

"Have a seat and let me—"

Porter slammed the door shut before I had a chance to finish. "I don't want a seat, Declan. I just want to know one simple thing."

He walked up until he was just a few inches away from me. His eyes were on fire, and the smell of his cologne was infused with sweat...and rage.

"Oh yeah," I replied, feeling like I was a speeding car that had lost control because I didn't even have the faintest idea of what was happening inside of me. "And what is that?"

"How could you do this?"

I scoffed. "I'm doing my job, Porter. I know that you're upset—I can see that clearly—but I need you to know that I didn't do this to hurt you."

His face tightened. "Then why did you do it?"

"Information came to me, and I simply reported on it," I said, trying to inject a calmness into my voice, which I hoped would help to deescalate him a little.

"These photos are an invasion of privacy. How did you even get them?"

"I'm not telling you my source, Porter." I was standing up to the man, but underneath my off-green baggy suit, I was trembling. I hoped he couldn't see it.

I also hoped that he couldn't tell that I totally agreed with him.

The photos *were* an invasion of privacy, taken by the Smiths' former neighbor, with a telephoto lens one evening. The sad truth was the Smiths weren't doing anything wrong. They were in the privacy of their bedroom—or at least, they thought it was private. And the neighbor, well, he was just a total pervert who got lucky and who knew a thing or two about uploading the images onto the dark web.

"I—I didn't want this to happen," I stammered.

I didn't. The brief I gave the hacker was to find something on the opposition, not more dirt on the mayor. But when he came back with what he had found on Mayor Smith, I had no choice. This was the story I had to report on.

It was Porter's turn to scoff. "Oh, really?"

"Yes, really." I reached out and tried to touch his forearm, but he pulled away sharply before I could.

"I can't believe you did this." His words felt like fingers around my throat, squeezing in tighter and strangling me.

"I never wanted to hurt you, Porter. You have to believe that." Please, please, *please* believe that.

"You could have given me a warning, a quick phone call to say, *hey, I'm just about to ruin a few people's lives, get ready.*" He started backing away from me. "That's all I wanted, Declan. If the situation was reversed, I would have done the same for you."

Tears filled my eyes. "Porter, I'm s—"

He opened the door and slammed it shut, disappearing before I had a chance to finish.

CHAPTER SEVENTEEN

PORTER

"Another drink?"

I looked up from my almost empty glass and was met with the smiling face of one of the bartenders. Pete, or Paul, or Patrick, or something. I knew all of Revolver's bartenders well, some of them *intimately* well, but this guy had only started recently, and my mind had been preoccupied with other things over the last few months.

"Sure," I said, forcing a smile. Because if alcohol couldn't make me feel better, then what would? The P-named bartender turned around and my eyes drifted down to his solid, tight ass that looked all sorts of good in his dark pants. But then a pang of guilt pummeled into my chest for checking the guy out. What the hell was that about?

It had been two days since the pegging story broke, and I was a complete mess. Work was a living nightmare with the press going off in a way I had never seen before. The story was getting national attention. And the level of vitriol and hatred spewed at the mayor, online and at our office, was out of control.

For a topic that most people probably hadn't even heard of, much less fully understood, it seemed that everyone suddenly had an opinion about pegging. One that they just had to share with the world. Most of it was the usual, bigoted vitriol. It amazed me that people could spout off about something they knew nothing about.

I got that anal sex was still one of the last remaining taboos. And a man getting fucked? Even if it was by a woman, or maybe *especially* because it was by a woman? Yeah, that was like the double cheeseburger of taboos.

I kind of got that, but what I couldn't wrap my brain around was why people were so quick to judge others. Why weren't they more willing to either shrug it off because it had literally nothing to do with them and didn't affect their lives in the slightest, or, if it did pique their interest, why didn't they look into it and maybe discover something they could explore themselves?

A loud yawn escaped from my mouth. I hadn't slept, eaten, or shaved since the story broke. I was wound so tight that every muscle in my body ached. I dragged my fingers across my stubbled chin as the bartender returned with my drink. "Thanks," I said, without looking up.

So I decided to come to the one place that had become like a second home to me over the years: Revolver. I was an active member of the community and had a number of acquaintances who, while they didn't feel like family, were at least familiar. My whole world had been rocked, and that's what I needed right now: familiarity and a feeling that I belonged somewhere in this crazy world. Even if that was at a BDSM club.

The sting of Declan's betrayal wasn't subsiding. I understood he had a job to do, and I wasn't trying to prevent him from doing it. But surely he could have called, heck, even emailed, to let me know the story? That was a common courtesy I would have expected any reporter in the city to extend to me.

But Declan clearly wasn't like any other reporter. As much as I hated to admit it, he had somehow managed to pierce through my defenses and into a part of me that I didn't let anyone into. And now I was stuck. My professional and personal worlds had collided—and clearly blown up—in the most spectacular of ways. I had no idea what my next move should be, on either front.

I looked around the place. It was pretty busy for a Thursday evening. I was sitting at the main bar, which was the place people would sit around and socialize. Around the central bar and heading off in each direction were the rooms where the action took place and the scenes unfolded. That wasn't what I came here for, though.

My thoughts drifted to my last time at the club, when I was also sitting by myself at the bar. I had to cancel my appointment with Declan that day due to a scheduling conflict on my part. I had to bring Josh here.

I met Josh at a ceremony honoring fallen soldiers on Veterans Day. He had fought in two tours: one in Iraq, the other in Afghanistan. A week before he was due to come back from his last tour, he stepped on a landmine. He almost lost his life, but he managed to escape with losing both legs. Due to nerve damage in his spine, he was in a wheelchair for life.

His story moved me on its own, but when he had shared that he was also into the kink lifestyle and that his injury had completely killed his sex life, I felt it was my duty to help him. So once a month, every month, for the last two years, I brought him to Revolver for an afternoon. It made him feel connected, like he was still a part of something. And it made me feel good, too, I had to admit, that I was doing my small part to help someone who had suffered through such a truly horrific experience.

For me, it proved that Revolver was more than just a BDSM club, a place where people came to meet others and delve into their fantasies. It really was a lifeline, a place where everyone belonged.

Getting kicked out of home at seventeen fucked me up. Badly. I still thought that, to this day, I carried some of those scars around with me. I mean, how could I not? The two people in the world whose only job was to love me couldn't do that. To them, I was a freak and an abomination. Someone not even worthy to live in their home with them.

But at Revolver, I had never encountered even the slightest judgment directed at me. People around here really were free to express themselves in whatever way they chose to.

And that's truly the beautiful thing about kink. It's not just the sex, although believe me, kinky sex was definitely the best kind of sex. It's the kindred spirits you meet. People who you might not have anything in common with sexually, other than a shared sense of open-mindedness. That created a deep connection between people who would otherwise have been complete strangers, which was a beautiful and rare thing, in a world that was so often divided and judgmental.

But as I took the scene in, I didn't feel that homey feeling I usually did. Instead, I felt...empty.

"Well, hello stranger."

I recognized the voice before I even turned around. It was Jeremy. "I thought I got lucky seeing you at the restaurant the other day, but this," he tugged at my sleeve, "is much more fortuitous."

We had played together on a number of occasions, and I had to admit, I had a good time with him.

"Oh, is it now?" I heard myself say, before regretting it almost immediately. The guilt was back, along with something else—a complete lack of desire for the guy.

And that wasn't Jeremy's fault at all. He was devastatingly attractive. He ticked all my boxes. Young. Well built. Smooth. Nice eyes. Kinky as hell. But for some reason, even as my mind searched to access the part of myself that liked those things, I was coming up with absolutely nothing.

I placed my hand over his fingers, which were creeping further up my arm, and pushed them away from me. A confused look washed over his eyes.

"Come on, Porter. Don't play hard to get," he said as he reached for the small of my back. I tensed up immediately at the touch.

He leaned in closer and breathed seductively into my ear. "I know how much you love my body, how much it drives you wild. You said it was perfect the last time you tied me up and fucked me senseless."

My jaw clenched so tight I thought my teeth would shatter into pieces. Technically, Jeremy was correct. I did remember saying that to him last time we hooked up. But all of a sudden, his perfect body—and the idea of perfect in general—didn't appeal to me anymore.

Being with Declan had shown me—well, truly, and beyond a shadow of a doubt—that beauty came in all shapes, sizes, and forms. Declan's self-consciousness in front of me when he undressed to come in for a swim was a thousand times more appealing to me than Jeremy's cocky boasting about his amazing body.

His hand travelled down my back, lower, until he pressed his fingers into my ass. "No," I said firmly as I stepped away. "I'm sorry, Jeremy, but I'm not interested."

A dark look fell over his face as he pursed his lips thinly. "Suit yourself," he said with a dismissive air that irritated the fuck out of me. He began to walk away. "Doms are a dime a dozen around this place, Porter. I can find someone else like that." And with a finger snap and a huff, he walked away, leaving me stewing at the bar.

Why had I come here? If I had thought, for even a minute, that a distraction fuck would get my mind off Declan, I had well and truly blown that theory out of the water with Jeremy. A young, hot, and normally just-my-type guy had practically thrown himself in front of me, and yet it didn't arouse me in the slightest.

I finished my drink and made my way to the door. Revolver wasn't the right place for me at the moment, and being there was only increasing my agitation, for some reason.

A nice hot shower, followed by a wank, sounded a thousand

times better. And that's what I had every intention of doing as I stepped out onto the street and ran smack bang into...Declan Davies.

"What the hell are you doing here, Declan? Are you following me?" I blurted out angrily.

Declan blinked a few times, as if he was just as surprised to see me as I was to see him. "Uh, no," he said slowly. "I live two blocks away from here. I was getting my groceries," he said as he raised the two brown paper bags he was holding.

I felt a little stupid for jumping the gun, but I wasn't going to apologize to him. "Oh, okay, then."

"Well," we both said at the same time.

We looked at each other awkwardly.

"Porter," he jumped in quickly. "Can we please talk? Come back to my place, and let's sit down and discuss things. Please." His hazel eyes were pleading with me. Damn it. I couldn't resist.

"Fine," I agreed coolly. After all, I still did need to have a professional working relationship with the guy.

But if Declan thought that there was anything that he could say to change my mind, he was seriously mistaken.

CHAPTER EIGHTEEN

DECLAN

"Come in, come in," I said as I waved Porter into my shoebox of an apartment. I looked around at the mess. Clearly, I hadn't been expecting company. The open-plan kitchen, living, and dining room was strewn with papers, clothes, empty takeout containers, and basically anything else that I had touched in the last two weeks. Cleaning wasn't exactly at the top of my priority list.

I studied Porter's face, trying to get an idea of what was going through the man's head as he looked around the small apartment. The whole place was the size of his entryway.

"Would you like a drink?" I offered with a smile.

"No," he replied flatly, removing a pile of newspapers from the loveseat, placing them on the coffee table, and sitting himself down.

I sat down in the recliner Mom had given me when I moved out, across the table from him.

He sank back a little further into the loveseat and crossed his legs. "You wanted to talk, Declan. So talk."

Right, okay, yes. I had him here. This was my chance to explain. And that's exactly what I wanted to do. I was going to tell Porter everything.

"I want to tell you the truth, Porter. You deserve to know."

He frowned, but a slight curiosity danced across his eyes. "Well, I'm listening."

His voice was still distant, but it was warming a little. Or at least I hoped it was. Or I could have been imagining things, who knew?

"This is all off the record and completely confidential," I began.

He nodded. "Of course."

Now that I had his undivided attention, I didn't know where to begin. I inhaled sharply.

"Firstly, I want to start by saying how sorry I—"

Porter raised his hand in the air. "Declan," he interrupted. "I didn't come here to hear your apologies or lame-ass explanations. If you can't tell me the truth, the *real* truth, then I might as well leave."

He began to get up.

"Wait, wait," I cried. "I'll tell you the truth. Just please don't leave. Please."

He looked at me strangely, and for a moment, I couldn't tell if he wanted to kill me or kiss me. As much as I was hoping for the latter, I had a sinking feeling it was actually the former.

He settled back into the seat and shot me an expectant and slightly impatient look.

I sat up a little straighter, and that's when a jolt of pain rocked my lower back. I grimaced as I readjusted the way I was sitting.

"Are you alright, Declan?"

I glanced over and saw Porter scanning me worriedly.

"I'm fine," I said, breathing through the pain. The last thing I wanted was his sympathy. I had never played that card in my life, and I wasn't about to start now.

After taking a few breaths, I was ready to continue. I looked across at Porter and blurted out the cold, hard truth. "Mayor Smith is my father."

Porter's pupils dilated, and he shook his head in disbelief. "Wait, what did you just say? Are you serious? Because if this is some kind of twisted joke, Declan..."

"I'm not kidding, Porter."

He was still clearly in shock, judging by the way his eyes weren't able to fix onto anything for longer than a few seconds. "I— I don't understand," he stuttered. "How are you the mayor's son? The man's only ever had two..."

"Jacqueline," we both said at the same time as our eyes met.

"You're Jacqueline's son?" Porter asked, still a little dazed, but I could see the pieces starting to come together in his mind.

"I am. She got pregnant with me in her first year in college. When she told him, he ended things with her."

"Oh my god." Porter's eyes were continuing to do their million-mile-an-hour thing. He looked up at me again. "So this is your revenge, then?"

I shook my head firmly. "No. It's not."

"Well, I kind of wouldn't blame you if it was. William did a really shitty thing to you and your mom. She must be really pissed."

"She's not."

Just as Porter was starting to regain his composure, his face crumpled in confusion again.

"Look, Porter, I know what this probably looks like to you. The mayor's illegitimate reporter son trying to take the man down by exacting revenge on him for abandoning his mother. Am I close?"

Porter shuffled a little in his seat. "Yeah, well, I mean, you're definitely in the ballpark."

"Well then, we're in completely different stadiums, Porter. My mom's not some bitter, scorned woman. And I'm not angry at the man. He did what he did. I think he's a total asshole for doing it, but that's not why I wrote the stories about him."

"So, you've never met him then?"

I shook my head from side to side. "Nope. I've tried. I reached out to him a couple of times, but he made it clear he wasn't interested, so I left it alone."

Porter's light green eyes had become even paler, and I suddenly noticed the clues of tiredness written across his face. His lightly stubbled jaw, the dark puffy circles under his eyes. "So tell me, Declan, why did you write the articles about him then?"

I leaned in closer. "For one simple reason. To tell the truth. I really hope you can believe me, Porter, because I swear to you, that is the truth."

He stared at me with such an intensity that I felt my skin flush with heat under his glare. A long silence filled the space between us. He looked away for a moment, taking in my meager apartment. What was he thinking? I would have donated my right testicle to research to have the faintest clue of what was going on in his mind.

Finally, he turned to face me and slapped his hands against his knees. "I do believe you, Declan. I know you well enough to know you're telling me the truth."

His words made me feel lighter, but not happy. Despite being so close to each other in my tiny living room, I'd never felt further away from him. While I was relieved that he believed me, I was scared that I had blown things up irrevocably between us. Would we ever be able to go back to what we had?

"I should go," he said standing up. My heart dropped in disappointment at the words. I didn't want him to leave. I wanted him to stay and tell me that we could still be together.

But then another thought pummeled into my chest with such force that I couldn't even stand up: were we even ever together in the first place?

As he reached for the door handle, he turned around to face me. "One more thing," he said softly. "What's happening to the article you're writing about me? Is that still going ahead?"

I nodded. "Yes, it is."

His lips tugged upward for the briefest of moments. "Alright then. Goodnight, Declan."

And just like that, he closed the door and left me alone.

CHAPTER NINETEEN

PORTER

The doorbell rang just as I was taking a sip of gin. I closed my eyes, letting my lips linger on the cold glass for just a second longer, before getting up off the couch. I padded over to the front door.

It had been a week since I had last seen Declan, although it felt like he had never left my mind at all during that time. All I could think about was him, the articles he had written about the mayor, and the article he was due to publish about me any day now.

But more than anything else, I couldn't get the expression he had on his face as I was leaving his apartment out of my head. It haunted me, following me wherever I went. Whenever I closed my eyes, I would see him sitting there, alone and afraid. It took every ounce of self-restraint I had in me not to do what I wanted to do so badly: go to him and protect him.

I couldn't do that because, in that moment, I had broken my cardinal rule, my strongest and most fiercely protected boundary.

My work life and my personal life had collided head-on, and like a plane with a bomb on it, there was no way it could end well.

I opened the door. "Hello, Declan. Come in, please."

"Hey, Porter," he said as he stepped in, and I did everything I could to suppress the flutter of happiness in my belly. I tried to convince myself that it was because he had gone home and gotten changed from what he was wearing during the day.

I saw him at the press conference that morning, dressed in perhaps his worst suit yet. Let's just say, even Don Johnson would have looked at that suit in the '80s and walked away from the creamy-caramel nightmare.

The media briefing had been the mayor's final one. He had officially resigned and the deputy mayor, Nathan Roberts, was stepping in to fill the vacancy.

The hungry pack of vultures had at least managed to restrain themselves a little. It was the first time since the pegging story had broken that it wasn't their main topic of questioning. The questions were mainly about the mayor's plans for the future, which he kept deliberately vague. I don't think the man knew himself what he was going to do next.

The main line of questioning directed at the new mayor was focused on his previous day's media release, where he remained ambiguous about whether he would be running at the next election in a few months. Which, of course, led the press to the next logical line of questioning: if not him, then who would be running in the next mayoral election?

I kept looking over at Declan, sitting there in the middle of the packed room in his frightfully ugly suit, but he never looked back at me. Not even once. I kept hoping he would look over, that our eyes would meet even momentarily, but it never happened.

The pegging story must have propelled Declan forward in his career, given that it went viral and led to some of the biggest reporters in the country descending upon Daylesford in the days that followed. That had been what he was wanting all along. I tried being happy for him, I really did, but the sadness of how things were left between us wouldn't leave, and it wouldn't let me.

And that was, in part, why I had called him and asked him to stop over at my place. The whole situation was a mess—the mayor's scandals, the fact that Declan was the reporter who broke them, and that I was the chief of staff who was meant to have stopped them.

And I didn't.

I had dropped the ball, and that was partly due to my feelings for him. I couldn't deny that simple truth anymore. I also couldn't continue like this, blurring the lines like we had been doing, between my professional and personal lives. It was tearing me apart inside.

"Can I get you anything?" I asked as we sat down on the sofa in my sunken living room.

"No, I'm all good, thanks." He flashed a friendly smile, so at least that was something.

"I need to talk to you, off the record." That term had started off so playfully between us, but now, it was laden with a heavy-duty seriousness.

His smile didn't waver. "Sure."

It had been on my mind the entire time since the pegging story came about, but it became even more real that morning, watching the mayor hand over the reins in front of the media.

He was out, and I had an in, but I also had one colossal sexual history that, if exposed, would make the current scandal look like a sweet Hallmark movie.

It was only as I was about to start talking that it hit me. Apart from people in the lifestyle who knew me and my three closest friends, he was the first person I would be sharing this part of myself with. I quickly grabbed my drink and took a sip. I needed that burning rush of alcohol against the back of my throat to will myself to speak.

"As you may or may not be aware, Declan, I have some future political ambitions."

He gave a slight nod. "I've heard a few things around the place. I didn't know if they were true, though."

"Well, they are. I'm not ready to make my intentions public just yet. It's still a little...."

"Soon?" he offered.

"Exactly." I grinned and felt a sense of warmth in my chest that we were on the same wavelength.

"Well, I'm sure you will make an excellent mayor, Porter."

Words that were meant to fill me with confidence had the exact opposite effect. My hands felt clammy, so I reached for the drink again. "I've got some dirty laundry I need to air out," I said and then swallowed down the rest of the drink, letting a few of the ice cubes fall into my mouth. I played with them between my teeth.

Declan narrowed his eyes. "Are you going to tell me?"

"Yes, I am."

"Why?"

"Because I want you to know, Declan."

"Why?"

"Because..." I sighed loudly. "Because the truth matters."

His gaze hit mine, and in that moment, a closeness returned between us that I realized had been missing for far too long.

"Go on." His tone was genial and yet a little guarded. Or maybe it was me who was being guarded, and I was just projecting it onto him. Who the fuck knew?

I could feel my heart racing and beads of sweat popping up all over my forehead. I swallowed hard.

"Declan," I began. "I have a bit of a past when it comes to..."

"Sex?" He said it so nonchalantly that it caught me off guard.

"Yes. How did you know?"

"There are rumors." He waved his hand in the air, until he saw the look on my face. "Nothing serious and no one knows *anything...*"

That wasn't true. He did. Declan knew more about me than any reporter should ever have known. Oh, what the hell. If I had to do it, I was going to go all in.

"Declan, I'm a Dom. A kinkster. I'm a part of the kink community. A very *active* part. Name the sexual activity, and there's a good chance I've done it. Probably more than once. Even one of my closest friends called me an amusement park of kink."

Declan's face remained the same, completely expressionless. I held off saying anything more, waiting for a reaction. But, nothing.

"Did you hear what I just said?" I finally asked, when I couldn't take the silence anymore.

"Yes," came the soft reply. Declan was looking down at the ground. "I figured."

"You did?" I felt a panic rising in my chest. I had shared the most private part of myself with him, and I wasn't able to get a read on the guy. What was he thinking? Feeling? Judging?

A sudden burst of shame filled me at the thought of him judging me.

"Yeah," he said quietly as he finally looked up at me. His face was soft, and his hazel eyes were warm. "I assumed that the moment you showed me the restraints that were permanently fixed to your bed. It kind of gave it away, Porter." He let out a half-smile in my direction and then cast his gaze at the floor again.

A small amount of stress left my body, but there was plenty more that didn't.

He knew. He finally knew. I felt a heady mix of relief and terror.

I had just confided my ultimate truth to the person who could end my entire career with just one article.

CHAPTER TWENTY

DECLAN

"You're not saying a lot."

I wasn't deliberately avoiding Porter, but there was no way I could bring myself to look at him. Until I heard the anguish in his voice.

I turned my head up and saw his eyes. He was breathing heavily and looked about as uncomfortable as I felt. Not because of what he had told me, that wasn't it at all. I half-suspected as much anyway. I might not have known all the details, but Porter had 'kinkster' written all over him. I didn't mind. If anything, it turned me on like crazy.

No, the thing that was bothering me was my own hypocrisy. I talked all the time about the importance of truth and bringing important information to light...about others. In reality, I couldn't even bring myself to tell Porter the truth about myself.

And if I wasn't drowning in my own pool of loser-ness, I would have gone over to him, kissed him, and told him how much he meant to me. But I couldn't even do that. I sat there on his sofa in some weird state of paralysis, unable to move or speak, which, as it turned out, was the last thing Porter needed. He looked like he was about to have a heart attack.

"Declan, are you okay? Say something, please. You're freaking me out."

"I don't mean to freak you out," I said, my voice as shaky as my fingers. "I just—I just...."

Before I knew it, Porter walked over to me and slipped his hand around my fingers. His touch instantly soothed me, and I felt the tension leave my shoulders. When I was finally able to look up at him, his eyes were filled with the last thing I was expecting.

Love.

I didn't deserve it, not after everything I had done. Even though I had my reasons, and I stood by them, the grace Porter was extending to me in that moment overwhelmed me. Without any ability to stop it, red-hot tears spilled from my eyes.

Porter pulled his hand away and stood up. When he returned a few moments later, through a tear-soaked gaze, I could see him handing me a box of tissues.

"Here, take these."

I grabbed the box and quickly pulled out a tissue, dabbing it against the corners of my eyes, hoping it would quash the tears that were still yet to fall. But no such luck. I continued to sob uncontrollably.

With the gentlest of care, I felt Porter reach his arms around me. He held me close, but not too tight, knowing it would hurt. That made me cry even more. I hadn't even told the man about my condition, and yet, here he was, factoring that into the way he looked after me.

I continued to cry, cradled in the safety and warmth of his arms. He delicately ran his fingers through my hair. "It's all good, Declan. Take all the time you need. I've got you, my sweet boy."

As the word fell from his lips, I felt his chest flinch slightly.

Was it an accident? Had it slipped out unintentionally? Or was it really what he was thinking and wanting?

It did something to my insides. Something that felt good and sunny and fuzzy, something I wanted to feel more of. But before I could, I had to stop crying and start talking.

At long last, I managed to compose myself. "Thank you for telling me, Porter," I said as I fought to blink away the tears.

"I needed to be honest with you," came his reply.

I chewed down on my lower lip. "And I need to be honest with you too."

"Only if you're ready."

At that moment, my heart burst, but I didn't know if it was from happiness or sadness. I didn't deserve him.

"I have scoliosis."

My statement hung heavily in the air between us.

Porter delicately brushed my cheek with the back of his warm fingers. He smiled as he spoke. "Well, as it turns out, you're not the only one who's good at figuring things out, Declan."

"You knew?" I asked, already knowing the answer myself.

"Not the specifics, of course. But I could see."

"And it doesn't bother you?"

"No." His reply was instant, definitive. But it was what he said next that truly shocked me. "Does it bother *you*?"

My breath caught in my throat. "Of course it bothers me. I'm in pain pretty much all the time, and I look...hideous. Like some deformed creature."

Porter's face grew serious. "I'm sorry that you're in pain. I can't even begin to imagine how hard that must be. But I will correct you on one thing, and if I have to, I'm prepared to fight you on it, Declan."

My heart thundered in my chest as I waited for him to keep talking. "You are not, and you never will be, hideous or a deformed creature. At least not to me."

He pressed his smooth fingers to my lips. "You've interrupted me before when I wanted to say it, and I don't want that to happen again. But you, Declan Davies, are the most beautiful boy I have ever laid my eyes on."

And with that, Porter removed his fingers and brought his soft lips to mine. I let out a low moan of pure need as I melted into the velvety kiss.

I didn't know what was happening, or why it was happening, or what it would mean. But in that moment, with his tongue playing with mine, I didn't care. I felt his fingers holding the back of my head, supporting me in exactly the way I needed.

I was falling hard for Porter Jones, and something inside me told me that whatever happened, he would be there to catch me.

CHAPTER TWENTY-ONE

PORTER

"Wait, you're fucking the reporter?"

I slammed my hands on the table, causing everyone's drinks to spill slightly. "Stirling," I exclaimed. "Don't be so...vulgar. That sounds like something—"

"That I would say?" Nick chimed in with a devilish grin, looking way prouder of himself than he should have been.

"Exactly, thank you, Nick." I flashed him a warm smile.

"Are you going to call it, Steel, or am I?" Stirling continued unabated. Mikey stood by his side and was looking up so lovingly at his Daddy, the man he had brought out of his shell, the man who was gearing up to give me the ribbing of a lifetime.

"I'll do it," Steel said with a laugh, as he pulled his boy, Nick, even closer to him. He brought his hand around his mouth, forming a makeshift mouthpiece. "We have officially entered Amber Alert territory, you guys. In twenty years of knowing him, this has never happened before. But ladies and gentlemen, and I do warn you to brace yourselves for this announcement—Porter Jones doesn't want to talk about sex."

I felt the heat of six pairs of eyes and more than a few suppressed giggles, zooming in on me. I looked around Deffers, but there was no escape.

"Can we please not talk about my sex life right now?" I said as I lifted my drink to my mouth. "Hudson and Liam are back." I beamed as I looked over at my newly returned friend. He looked so happy, so tanned, so muscular, and so very much in love.

"I'm sure you guys have much more interesting stories to fill us all in on."

"No, no," Hudson giggled. The three-hundred-pound walking wall of muscle was giggling. What alternate universe were we living in? "This sounds way more interesting than anything we've been up to these last few months."

I bristled slightly at the lack of support from my friend. "I highly doubt that," I said, shooting him a *please save me* look, which he proceeded to completely ignore. "We've only been travelling around the country and having mindblowing, multi-orgasmic sex with one another, not with the reporter who broke two of the biggest political scandals of the year."

"Well," I cleared my throat. "When you put it like that."

The group laughed, and as I looked around, it was so good to see everyone back together again for the first time since Hudson and Liam had taken off on their cross-country adventure.

I also couldn't help but be struck by the fact that each of my three friends had found their boy. They were all happily in love and, as a result, happier in life.

I was the last single Daddy standing. And while that didn't surprise me in the slightest, the niggling feeling in the base of my stomach that said I didn't want to be single anymore did.

"We have done a little more than just have out-of-this-world sex," Liam said as he began to fill us in on all of the work he had been doing highlighting important environmental issues. It included attending conferences where he spoke about the effect of climate change on farmers and in the agricultural sector *right now*, not at some distant point in the future. He also filled us in on a number of the protests and rallies they had attended, in the hopes of highlighting environmental issues to more people, especially younger people, and encouraging them to get actively involved.

I listened to what he was saying, but my mind kept drifting back to thoughts of Declan. And my friends' inevitable return to him. There was no way they would let it slide without more conversation—and more ribbing.

But the truth was, I didn't really know what to tell them.

Two days had passed since Declan and I had opened up to each other. Apart from the odd glance during the daily press conference, which I was happy to say he was now returning, our paths hadn't really crossed again.

But they would later tonight. I had invited Declan over to my place after drinks with these guys. And let's just say I wasn't really in the mood for talking. My cock started to stiffen in my pants at the thought of Declan tied up, naked on my bed. But what really sent my heart into overdrive was the thought of talking to Declan about a contract.

"We have some news too," Mikey squealed excitedly once Liam was done filling us in.

"Ooh, do tell," Nick replied with just as much enthusiasm.

I smiled. I really did like the energy the boys brought to the group. It was different and an adjustment, of course, but it was like one of those things that you never expected, but then once you had it, you couldn't ever imagine your life without it again.

"Can I tell them, Daddy?" Mikey looked up and batted his lashes at Stirling.

"Of course you can, Mikey boy." Stirling pressed his lips to Mikey's forehead, and yeah, it was all sickly sweet and all, but damn, if it didn't tug at a long-held longing in my heart.

"We're going to have a baby!" Mikey cried out, unable to control the volume or pitch of his voice.

"Well, we're going to start *trying*," Stirling clarified as everyone jumped out of their seats and leaped onto the guys in a tangle of hugs and back slaps.

"That's such good news, you guys," I said. "I always knew Stirling had powerful swimmers. If anyone's sperm could get another man pregnant, it's his."

The group erupted in laughter.

"Seriously, though," Steel said once we had all settled down a bit. "Which route are you guys going down, adoption or surrogacy?"

"Both, actually," Stirling replied. "We just have so much love to give, we don't really mind which way our perfect child comes to us."

"And we figure if we choose both options, it doubles our chances, you know?" Mikey added.

"Sounds like a good strategy, guys," Hudson said and we all nodded in agreement.

"Well, cheers," I said, lifting my glass. "To Stirling and Mikey. May your journey to finding your family be a smooth and easy one."

"Hear, hear." A cacophony of glasses clinking filled the air.

A short silence fell over the group. Hudson turned to Steel. "And how are you guys doing?"

If I was feeling panicked about the group wanting to drill me about Declan, Steel was looking how I was feeling.

"Things are good," Steel said warmly, but I knew that professional game face of his. There was a world of stuff going on between him and Nick.

I'd only had the chance to text Steel a few times, given the shitstorm that I was dealing with at work, but from what I had gathered, he and Nick were starting to talk more openly to one another. That was a good sign, and exactly what they needed to be doing.

Bringing in a new element to a relationship, like age play, required *Gilmore Girls*-levels of talking. But I had a good feeling about those two. They'd find a way to work through it and build the relationship they both wanted.

I suggested they go to Revolver and meet other Daddies and littles in a social environment as a first step. Steel said he would talk the idea over with Nick.

Picking up on the slight awkwardness, as was the man's sixth sense, Hudson then turned the conversation back to me. Great.

"Alright, Mr. Jones," he said, totally stealing my whole *drumming fingers on the table* move. "We've told you what's been happening with us, and so has everyone else, which now leaves you."

"Actually," I said, looking down at my watch. "Speaking of leaving, I'm late."

Stirling's eyebrow shot up. "Late to what?"

"Late for sex," I replied as casually as I could, reaching for my jacket.

"Sex with Declan?" Steel asked curiously.

"Of course. Who else would I be having sex with?"

Damn it. I'd said too much. "Look, guys. I'll fill you in when I know more myself, alright? At the moment, my head is spinning, and my heart doesn't know what the hell is going on."

"And your dick is feeling left out," Stirling joked, and the group laughed.

"Stirling," I exclaimed for what felt like the millionth time that night. "Stop being so...trashy."

"Porter, you have literally given us every last graphic detail of your sex life for years. Right down to the number of cocks you've been able to take up your ass at any one time," Stirling said, putting me in my place.

He was right. I had done that. But for some reason, I didn't want to talk about Declan. At least, not yet.

"Maybe Porter just needs some time?" Hudson suggested in that gentle way of his. God, how I had missed him.

"How long are you guys in town for?" I asked, looking over at the man as I made my way around the group, giving everyone a quick goodbye hug.

"Just a few days," he replied.

"Well, maybe we can catch up again?" I suggested.

"For sure," he replied as his face broke out into the widest smile I had ever seen.

"When we're not having mindblowingly brilliant sex, that is," Liam added as he laughed and pulled himself even closer to Hudson.

"Or when you're not," Hudson added goodnaturedly.

He looked at me, and like a fifteen-year-old schoolkid, I blushed a bright beetroot red.

The man had no idea.

CHAPTER TWENTY-TWO

DECLAN

"What's—what's this?" I asked, looking down at the piece of paper Porter had just handed to me.

"It's a contract, Declan."

I lifted my head to meet his gaze. He looked...pensive. I mean, drop-dead gorgeous, as always, but he had an uncharacteristic nervous vibe about him as well. He even shuffled uncomfortably a little as he readjusted himself on the sofa.

I'd been looking forward to coming over to his place all day. Ever since we'd had our last conversation and opened up to each other—him about his kink, me about my condition—something big had shifted within me.

I always knew I felt something toward him, but I didn't know exactly what it was. Or maybe if I did, I just wasn't ready to admit it to myself. But I was now. I was ready. I was falling for the man.

The man whose eyes now turned expectant as he looked at me. Oh right, I was meant to be looking at whatever he had just given me. I turned my attention to the piece of paper in my hand, and instantly, my breath hitched in my throat as I saw the words scrawled across the top of the page: *BDSM Contract.*

"Have you ever seen one of these before?" Porter's voice was soft and gentle, almost as soft and gentle as his touch. I felt his fingers gently graze my forearm, instantly filling me with a reassuring warmth.

"No." I said it with a sense of embarrassment, as if I should have seen one before. I mean, sure, I had heard about them, but John had never brought up the idea of a contract. Not even once. I guess I assumed they were something that happened in movies, not in real life.

"Well, don't feel too bad," Porter said as he stroked up and down my arm, his touch so soft it barely touched my arm hairs. "I've never done one of these myself, either."

I looked at him, puzzled. "You haven't?"

He blushed slightly.

"Sorry, I didn't mean to sound so surprised," I added hastily. "It's just that you're so... experienced. I mean, you even said it yourself that you've pretty much done everything at least once, right?"

"Right." This time, it was Porter's voice that carried the slightest hint of embarrassment. "I have done pretty much everything when it comes to sex. But never...this."

"Why not?"

The directness of my question seemed to surprise him a little, but he simply squared his shoulders and took a moment to think about it. When he was ready to speak, he said, "I guess I've just never found the right boy."

His gaze lingered on me, and I felt my face—no, my entire body —flaming with a flush of desire. "And you have now? Found the right boy, that is?" Despite what it may have sounded like, I wasn't fishing for a compliment. Heck, I could barely string a question together. I genuinely wanted to know whether he was being serious. This was something too important to get mixed up in a miscommunication between us.

"I have," he said, but for some reason that made his face tighten and his jaw clench.

"Then why the serious face?" I asked with a smile.

He didn't smile back. "Well, because, me liking you is... complicated, to say the least. You know what I'm talking about."

I nodded silently. I knew exactly what he was talking about, and I hated the situation that we were in. Mom's advice was proving to be true, and I was trying my best to follow it, but doing the right thing in such murky waters was not an easy path to navigate.

"Which is why I think a contract would actually be a really good thing for us," he said, relaxing his shoulders just a little.

I was definitely curious and open to it. I just needed to know more. "How so?"

"Well," he began as he sat up a little taller, "for starters, it establishes clear rules, limits, boundaries...and punishments."

Ooh, my cock twitched at that last word for some reason. I'd always been keen to explore punishment play, but I never had the level of trust I needed in someone to do that.

"Go on."

"And I think that in our very unique situation, that sort of a framework, where we define what our relationship is, and the goals and parameters that guide and define it, would work."

I nodded again. Everything he was saying was not only making sense, but it was also resonating deeply within me. This was something that I wanted and needed. A clear, upfront structure where we could both say what we were looking for. I could only imagine how good that would feel to have something like that in place.

"I'm going to be honest with you, Declan. I've always had very clear boundaries in place in my life. There was work, and there was my private life. There was never any blurring of those lines...until you."

"Me?"

He relaxed even more as his lips tugged upward at the corners. "Yes, you," he said playfully. "With your beautiful face, that lower lip I could nibble on forever, your ugly-ass suits, your nerves of steel, and legs of a baby deer—especially after a few margaritas. I've never met anyone like you before, Declan. And I'm..." He cleared his throat. "I'm falling for you."

My heart was jumping for joy inside my chest, and I was pretty sure I was grinning like an idiot as well, but I couldn't help it. Hearing those words from Porter hit me in all the right places. The best bit was that I felt exactly the same way in return.

"So while I think a contract would be great for us in our personal relationship, I think it would actually help us in defining the boundary around our professional relationship as well."

"Yeah, that makes sense," I said.

"We both need to have an opportunity to work on this together. What I've given you is a very, very early first draft. I just wrote down a few things that popped into my head. For me, as I told you before, I'm interested in being a Dom outside of the bedroom as well. But I need you to really consider that and talk to me about what you're comfortable with, okay?"

"That sounds great." My voice was a heady mix of excitement and relief.

"So," he continued in that rich, relaxed tone of his. "Let's take some time to think about it and maybe meet up again to discuss things in more detail. How does that sound, Declan?"

"Fucking perfect." I winced. Dammit, that was my inside voice.

His lips stretched wide, and his eyes bulged out unevenly. God, could this moment get any more perfect? And then, Porter being Porter, it did.

"Now, Declan," he said as he took the contract out of my hand and placed it on the coffee table. His eyes had transformed from adorable to filled with a burning lust. "I did buy some new equipment, and it arrived just this afternoon. What do you say we give it a test run?"

"Tell me more about this *equipment*," I said, running my hand down his hard chest, stopping just above his belt buckle.

A dirty smile stretched his lips. "I have a better idea, Declan. Why don't I show you?"

Ten minutes later, I had both wrists strapped to Porter's bed and was lying there naked and waiting for him. "Come on, Porter. What are you doing in there?" I yelled out. He had disappeared into the en suite bathroom a few minutes ago, and I was starting to get a little impatient and very, *very* horny. Being tied up did that to me.

I didn't hear anything, but a few moments later, he entered the room. My eyes practically fell out of their sockets. If Porter Jones looked good in a custom-made three-piece business suit, then the man was nothing short of stunning perfection in a black leather harness and matching jockstrap.

"Whoa," I said. It was the only word my brain was able to come up with.

Porter walked over to me. Slowly. Seductively. Each step raised my heartbeat even more until I thought I would explode with anticipation. The leather harness clung to his shoulders and chest, accentuating both the hardness of his muscles and the suppleness of his skin.

I wanted to touch him, taste him, but I couldn't. I was tied up. Just like how he wanted me to be. And that thought drove me out-of-my-mind crazy...in the best possible way.

"Is this the equipment you were talking about before?" I asked, once at least some blood had returned to my brain.

"Oh no," he said, flashing me a wicked grin as he reached the foot of the bed. "This is the equipment I was talking about."

He leaned over and picked something up from the floor which I couldn't see. He placed it in both hands and then stretched his arms out toward me. I still didn't know what it was exactly. It looked like a three-foot black bar of some sort.

"What is that?" I asked.

"This," he said, bouncing the bar in his hands, "is a spreader bar. I can use it for your ankles. Let's just say it gives me the access that I need."

"Oh, does it now?" I replied with a cheeky smirk. "See, here's the thing, though, Porter. The internet has completely ruined my imagination. I might need you to...show me."

His face lit up. "I've never been happier to hear those words. But before we get started. Do you remember the safeword?"

"Of course. McBeal."

"Good," he said firmly, his voice a heady combination of lust with an underlying note of concern. "And you will use the safeword the second you want me to stop. Correct?"

"Correct. *Sir.*"

Holy shit. I had no idea where that word came from. It just slipped out, totally unplanned. We'd never even talked about what to call each other, and yet it just came to me. And *out* of me.

I looked down the length of my body and could see the bulge in his jockstrap expanding. The leather pouch was no match for his erection. He was hard. I was making him hard. Seems like calling him *Sir* wasn't such a bad thing after all. My body flooded with desire at the thought, and I let it wash over me.

Porter delicately wrapped his fingers around my ankles and, with utmost care, moved my feet into place, just slightly wider than hip-width distance apart. He reached for the bar and placed it onto the bed. One at a time, he placed each ankle into the leather straps. The back of my calves pressed against the cold bar, and I shivered.

His face tensed. "Are you okay?" He stopped what he was doing and stared intently at me.

"I'm fine," I said, grinning. "The bar is a little cold. It just caught me by surprise, that's all."

Porter readjusted himself so that he was holding the bar with one hand, and with the other, he began to rub his hand up and down at the backs of both of my calves, trying to heat them up.

I kept grinning. The gesture was more symbolic than anything else, and even if it didn't warm my calves up, it sure as hell melted my heart.

The fact that he cared so much about me, and that my comfort was his top priority, made me feel like I would explode with joy. No other person had ever made me feel that way before, because no other man had ever taken the time, the effort to dedicate himself to my pleasure like Porter was doing.

Once he stopped rubbing the backs of my legs, he moved my ankles into position and clipped them into place against the bar. With two loud clicks, my feet were secured firmly in place.

"There, how's that?" he said, as he inspected his handiwork. He dragged his eyes from my legs suspended in the air, along my torso, and to the edge of my hands wrapped in restraints at the corners of the bed.

I closed my eyes to really tune in to the sensations going through my body. How did it feel? It was the first time my entire body was completely restrained. At first, I was worried that having my legs in the air would be painful or awkward. But so far, at least, it wasn't.

In fact, having my legs up in the air pushed more pressure onto my back, which was supported by the solid, firm mattress I was lying on. I actually felt more secure and comfortable in this position than when I was simply lying on the bed normally.

I took a few breaths. "I'm good. What about you, Porter?"

I was more concerned about him. Even though my legs would naturally hold the bar in position, since I didn't have a lot of lower body strength, I would need him to hold it in place.

"What do you think I have these guys for?" he said with a wicked smile as he proudly flexed both biceps for me. The sight took my breath away. For the first time, I was seeing a different side to Porter. He was a Dom—strong, confident, sexy as fuck—totally in his element.

"Are you ready?" he asked.

I nodded. "Yes."

"So what I'm going to do now, Declan, is raise your feet up. I'll go slow, and I need you to tell me if you are in pain at any time, okay? Use the safeword whenever you need to."

"I will," I panted. I didn't know if he was drawing it out on purpose, but my body was trembling with anticipation. I was ready. I was *more* than ready.

Slowly, and with all the care in the world, Porter raised my feet up into the air. His biceps bulged as he brought the bar up higher and higher, bringing my body into an L-shape.

Now I really got it. This was the perfect position. I was completely tied up, with both of my wrists and ankles restrained, and yet Porter had clear and direct access to my ass.

"I'm ready for you to fuck me," I said as Porter positioned the bar across his chest, my feet dangling out past his shoulders.

"Oh, I'm not going to fuck you tonight, Declan," he said as my heart sank.

"Why—why not?"

"Because I have something way better in mind. Do you trust me?"

That word barreled into my chest. I started panting loudly, before I was able to compose myself. "Yes."

That wasn't good enough for Porter.

"Declan." His voice was stern. "Are you sure you trust me?"

"Yes." I responded quicker and more loudly that time.

Porter gave a quick head nod and then, with that, began to kiss, and caress, and touch, and lick, every square inch of my body. He lowered and raised the bar every few minutes so that my legs wouldn't get pins and needles from being suspended in the air. Every time he did, he checked back in with me. At first, I was able to say *yes*, but after the fifth— or was it the sixth time?—my brain, like the rest of my body, had turned to mush.

Whatever disappointment I had felt about Porter not fucking me quickly dissipated. While I might not have had his cock inside me, I had the rest of him all around me, exploring the surface of my skin with an alternating mix of gentle tenderness and hungry need that made me feel more beautiful, more alive, more wanted, than I had ever felt in my entire life.

Surrendering my body to him was just the start. I couldn't wait to totally submit to this man in all other aspects of my life.

I was so fucking ready.

CHAPTER TWENTY-THREE

PORTER

"How does it feel?"

I pondered the new mayor's question as I looked around the old mayor's empty office.

"Surreal," I replied, looking at the man. He gave me a knowing nod, but said nothing more.

Nathan Roberts was a former teacher who ran for councilor in order to improve the city's education system. While Daylesford had some of the best private schools in the entire country, there was a gigantic gap when it came to school results in lower-income areas. Those schools underperformed the national average by a significant margin. But over the last ten years, and largely due to Nathan's tireless work in the area, that gap had been almost completely closed.

I enjoyed a good working relationship with him, but I didn't know him well on a personal level at all. So I had stopped by his office that morning, with a potted plant welcome gift in hand, to try and change that. I needed to get to know him a little better.

I had heard rumors he was going to retire at the end of the term, but I didn't know that for certain. And I had no idea what the man thought of me or whether he would be supportive of my efforts to run for mayor.

"Just over there," he said. I looked up and saw two moving men carrying boxes into the room. "Leave it all in the corner please, and I'll go through it later."

He glanced over at me and smiled. "The joys of moving, right?"

"Right." I studied the man. He was in his early sixties and looked affable in that white-bread inoffensive way.

"Let me guess, you probably have some questions for me."

"Yeah, just a few."

We both grinned.

He looked like he was going to say something, when the moving men returned with even more boxes.

"I've got an idea," he said, turning back to face me. "How about we go get a terrible coffee downstairs, and we can talk a little more privately?"

I nodded in agreement, and a few minutes later, we were sitting at a corner table at the café on the ground floor of our building.

"This really is terrible coffee," I said after I took my first sip. "I knew I had been avoiding this place for a reason."

He let out a small laugh. "It is shockingly bad, yes. But as a result, the place is almost always empty."

I looked around the café and saw that he was right. There was hardly anyone sitting in here.

I took another sip, but pushed it away as soon as I was done. The coffee was seriously undrinkable. Good thing I had ordered a soda as well, so I could at least wash the bad taste out of my mouth.

"You want to know if I'm running in the next election, don't you, Porter?" he asked bluntly. I liked that about the man. He was direct, and there was no BS with him. He called it like he saw it.

"Well...yeah," I said with a slightly sheepish nod. "Was I really that transparent?"

He grinned, but his eyes remained warm. "It's okay, Porter. There's nothing wrong with a man who has ambition. And I've been watching you. You're a good operator. You work hard. You're smart and on top of everything you need to be. You're passionate and doing this for all the right reasons. And...you're loyal."

A gust of guilt swept through my body. I reached for the coffee and drank it, like it was some form of punishment. I knew I hadn't done anything wrong. I didn't have a role to play in any of the two scandals that had afflicted Mayor Smith. That wasn't who I was. I would never exploit someone's sexuality or sexual preferences, in order to get ahead.

But I had become too close, too entangled with Declan. And he was the reporter behind the two stories that ended the mayor's career. Which, if nothing else, at least gave the impression that somehow, I was involved. I knew how the game worked. I had played it for long enough myself. In politics, optics were everything.

Mayor Roberts continued. "I know how close you and Mayor Smith were. And I have a sense of your ambition as well. And I have to say, I think you balanced your loyalty and your personal goals well, Porter."

"Thank you. It's nice to hear that. Part of me feels bad that the mayor's downfall potentially opens up a path for me, you know? I mean, assuming you don't—"

"I don't," he said firmly. "I have absolutely no intention of running for mayor at the next election."

"Can I ask why?"

He let out a long breath. "I'm ready to retire, Porter. Well, that's the answer I'll give publicly, and for the most part, it's true."

"What's the real answer, then?"

He looked at me, and I saw a twinkle in his eye. "I like you, Porter. You're as direct as I am."

We both snickered at the backhanded compliment.

"The truth is," he continued, "politics has gotten nasty. Real nasty. Look, don't get me wrong, it was always cutthroat. If you want an industry that's all roses and rainbows, go be a florist or something, you know?"

I raised my eyebrows, smiling in agreement.

"But these last few years, it's just become...brutal. The lack of even basic decency and respect is too much for me. I don't want to have anything to do with it anymore. Besides, I've achieved pretty much everything that I set out to, so I'm going to leave at the end of this term and end on a high."

That all made sense. "I can understand where you're coming from. And I agree with you. Politics has gotten dirtier than ever—"

"Which is why," he interrupted, "I'd have no problem endorsing you, Porter."

I pinched my brows tightly. "What do you mean?"

"You're clean as a whistle. You've got no skeletons in your closet. Heck, even the fact that you're in your forties and unmarried seems to work in your favor. I can't think of a better candidate for the position, Porter."

I took another sip of the godawful coffee, hoping the taste would put out the feeling of dread that was forming in my gut. I wasn't clean. At all. And that thought churned in my belly until I thought I would be sick.

I dragged my fingers through my hair. Mission one for the day had gone well. I knew Mayor Roberts had my back.

But mission two was going to be a lot more difficult. I had to talk to Declan and tell him how I felt. And I needed, more than anything else, his assurance that what I had shared about myself to him would never, ever be made public.

~

Later that night, after another brutally long day at the office, I stopped by Declan's apartment. I called ahead, of course, but I made it clear that I wanted to see him to talk, not for sex.

"Hey." His whole face lit up as he opened the door.

"Hey yourself," I said, as he leaned in and we kissed. His soft lips felt so good against mine. I closed my eyes and felt his hands run across my chest and down my stomach, grabbing my belt buckle with a teasingly rough pull.

I opened my eyes and gently pushed his hand away. "Perhaps you should invite me in? I'm not sure your neighbors would appreciate the little show you seem to want to put on."

"The neighbors would be fine," Declan murmured, still enamored with our kiss, more than in what I was saying.

I pulled away and walked past him, into his apartment. "Well, you're no fun," he teased as he walked in behind me, closing the door.

"I am plenty of fun," I said, turning around to be met with Declan practically throwing himself against me. He cupped the back of my neck, interlacing his fingers as he pulled me in for another kiss. It was even hungrier than before and held the promise of more to come.

How could I resist his warm body so close to mine? It felt so good, like a warm bath after a long day—which, come to think of it, didn't sound like such a bad idea.

I managed to free my lips from his for just a moment. "Have you got a bath?"

He stopped kissing me, his hazel eyes peering at me curiously.

He spoke slowly. "Yes. Why?"

"I could really do with one," I said, letting out a tired sigh.

"It wasn't what I was expecting," he said, placing the tip of his finger on my nose, "but since I like seeing you naked, I'll go run it."

I gave him a cheeky slap on the ass as he left.

Declan's bath was pretty much like the rest of his apartment:

the size of a dollhouse. But somehow, the two of us managed to get ourselves into it, even if it meant our knees were sticking out and our feet were pressed into each other's behinds.

"This is...cozy." It really wasn't, but I was alone with him, and whenever we were together, I always felt better. Even when I had something difficult I needed to talk about.

I tried to relax my shoulders, but they were firmly pressed against the tap that was jutting out of the wall. I readjusted my position, leaning a little more to the left, and that felt a little better.

"So, when you called, you said you wanted to talk?"

"I do. We need to."

He tilted his head. "About us? About the...contract?"

I nodded. "Bingo."

I looked around the tiny bathroom as I tried to put into words what I was feeling.

"I'm—I'm..."

"Confused?" Declan suggested.

I returned my eyes to him. "Yes. That's definitely part of it. How did you know?"

He let out a half-laugh. "Uh, because you're not the only one feeling it. How do you think this whole thing between us is making me feel? I'm a reporter, and you're chief of staff to the mayor. Talk about a conflict of interest."

I mulled over his words and felt silly for not considering his side of things in all of this. I'd been so wrapped up with what had happened to Mayor Smith, and the implications of that on my own career, that I didn't really consider the complications it created for Declan. This would be a good time to explore those...and maybe, at the same time, get answers to some of my own questions, too.

"Well, how are you feeling, then?" I asked. "In addition to being confused, that is."

Declan took a deep breath as he considered his response. He brought his fingertips to my exposed knees as he said, "Well, I *was* feeling confused and torn for a really long time..."

I waited. I could tell there was more coming, he just needed some time to find the right words. "I mean, I want to make it as a reporter and write stories about things that matter, you know? If I have to cover another fucking flower show, I think I'll scream."

We both laughed, the sound echoing loudly off the tiled bathroom walls.

"But there's a huge conflict there...with you. Even if you don't fully believe me, Porter, I never wanted to expose Mayor Smith like this. I hate that the stories about him were of such a private, sexual nature. Especially since I'm a...and well, you're a..."

The unspoken words floated between us, filling the tiny bathroom. As I looked at him, I believed him. It couldn't have been easy for him 'as a boy' to veer into a story that was filled with kink, and the kind of kink that most people misunderstood, at that.

And even though Mayor Smith probably never believed me, I felt for the man. It was like the pain, embarrassment, and shame that he felt were all feelings that weren't far from the surface for me, too. I could access them all too easily.

At least the only time that I had been exposed was in the privacy of my parents' house and not in front of the entire world. I couldn't even begin to imagine the sheer awfulness of what that must have felt like for him and his wife.

And I knew that it was never Declan's intention to unleash that sort of pain on them. He was just doing his job. It just so happened that it was a really shitty story that he had to write. But if he did it once, would he do it again? Would he write a story like that, a scandalous sex exposé, about...me?

"You said *was* before," I said, staring into his beautiful hazel eyes. "That you *were* feeling confused and torn. Has that changed for you?"

He nodded emphatically. "It has. Ever since you gave me the contract to look over, I've been thinking about it. And I've made a decision, Porter." The rigidness in his tone startled me, as did the tap that was pressing against my back. I ignored the pain and leaned over to the right this time.

"What about?"

"My story about you."

My heart started thundering. This would be it, this would be me finding out the fate of my future. It was all in Declan's hands.

"Don't worry," he said with a soft smile as he continued tracing his fingertips across my knees. "This...us...the fact that you're a Dom—I'll never publish it. And I'm willing to put that into our contract."

I let out a heavy breath I hadn't realized I was holding. "Thank you, Declan." I was beyond relieved, but for some reason, Declan wasn't looking as happy as I felt.

"What's wrong?" I asked.

"Nothing, apart from the fact that I'm the world's biggest hypocrite. I mean, I'm the guy who exposed the mayor, but I won't expose you because I like you. That's not exactly fair, now, is it?"

I winced. It wasn't fair or right, and there was no use in pretending otherwise.

"It's not, Declan. But we don't live in a world that accepts things that it should accept. If we did, none of these things would be an issue. The mayor could get pegged by his wife, I could be a Dom, and it could all be out in the open."

My mouth felt dry, but I could feel the adrenaline coursing through my veins as I spoke. My internal defense system had been tripped.

"But there are still too many people in the world who look at these things with judgment, scorn, or even worse, such vile contempt that it can really hurt a person. That's why we have to...hide." My voice cracked on that last word.

It broke something deep inside of me that, as a man in his forties, I still had to hide who I was. And that I would probably have to hide for the rest of my life.

It was funny. I had gotten the answer that I wanted from

Declan, confirmation that he wouldn't out me as a kinkster, but for some reason, the relief that brought me was fleeting.

Now, I was just an oversized man in a small bathtub, with a tap stubbornly pressing against my back.

"Come on, let's get outta here," I said to Declan. "The water's getting cold."

CHAPTER TWENTY-FOUR

DECLAN

I tossed and turned all night after Porter left.

Our bathtime discussion turned out to be the ultimate boner-killer. I had hoped that he'd be up for something more than just talking when he called to say he wanted to come over. But after we got out of my cramped, cold bath and had dried ourselves off, he left pretty much straight away.

I guess I couldn't blame him, really. I was feeling pretty crappy myself. I never set out to take down the mayor of Daylesford, and I sure as hell never intended to start falling head over heels—or restrained wrists over spreader bar-strapped ankles, in this case—for the chief of staff.

Like Porter had said, life wasn't fair.

But sometimes, and usually when you least expected it, life could strike you with the most wonderful inspiration.

I finally got up just before four and padded over to the kitchen to get a drink of water. That's when it hit me like a bolt of lightning.

Well, except for the whole *dying after getting hit by lightning* bit. No, I was struck by an idea so awesome it made me feel more genuinely excited about my work than I had been in a very long time.

In addition to writing for *The Daylesford Times*, I also freelanced under a few different pen names for other online publications and blogs. Writing under a different name, and to a different audience, allowed me to explore and express parts of myself that I couldn't tap into when I was Declan Davies, aspiring political reporter.

One hugely popular site I wrote for was called *Connect Kink*. It was an online community for people in the kink scene, ranging from those who were seasoned with decades of experience under their leather belts to complete newbies who had read a fifty shades of something book and wanted to check things out themselves. It didn't matter who you were or where you fit on the kink spectrum. Everyone was welcome, and everyone's voice was valid.

I blogged for them under the name Firecracker Frankie. Hey, when you created a fake author name, no one said it had to be realistic. And it was at four in the morning, standing over my kitchen sink, that my latest idea for a Firecracker Frankie article took hold.

I shaved, showered, and got ready for work in record time. It was still dark as I swiped my way into the building, carrying my personal laptop under my arm. I rubbed my hands in glee as I opened the laptop at my desk and waited for it to boot up.

The plan was simple. I would publish Porter's puff piece as planned for *The Daylesford Times*. It would be a glowing portrayal of the charming, charismatic, soon-to-be mayoral candidate. He really did do a lot of good work, especially with all of his volunteering, so it wasn't like I was making any of the stuff up. I was just showcasing one side of the man and not giving the whole picture.

And I could live with that because Firecracker Frankie was a whole other story. For *Connect Kink,* I could write the article that I really wanted to. One where I could explore the details of my own experience, while also pointing out the blatant hypocrisy that still existed in our society when it came to the acceptance of kink. There would be no real names used, of course, but I would draw on things that I had been through and knew about to flavor the article with the genuine authenticity it required.

I was buzzing on such a natural high that I didn't even need caffeine. As the sun rose and its glow spread across the floor, and more and more people came into the office, my fingers continued flying across two keyboards. The kink article was like rocket fuel for my puff piece, and when I got sick of writing the puff piece, I returned back to the kink article. I couldn't believe it, but by the time I looked at the clock on the wall, it was quarter to twelve, and I had finished both pieces. Damn, I was good.

"Declan."

I spun around in my chair and saw Lane and oily-faced Neil standing at the edge of my cubicle. Oh shit, that's right. They wanted to take me out for another business lunch today. My stomach grumbled as I realized I hadn't stopped writing, even to have breakfast.

"Are you ready to go?" Lane said, offering a somewhat friendly smile.

"Yes, I'm starving," I said as I put my wallet into my top drawer. I had learned my lesson from last time. This lunch, they were paying, and this time, we were eating.

"Why have you got two laptops?" Neil asked, stepping in a little closer.

"One's for my personal writing," I explained as I snapped that laptop shut. "The other one is for official work."

His lips stretched into a sneer. "You still freelance?" He tried to make it sound like the scummiest thing in the world and completely beneath him. I guess when you earned the kind of money that he did, it probably was. But I wasn't in the mood to bite or allow him to make me feel bad.

"I do," I said, getting up. I wasn't ashamed of it. The only thing that sucked was that some of my best writing was under a fake name.

I brushed straight past his scorn-filled, greasy face and said to Lane, "I need to eat. Stat. Let's go."

I came back from lunch a respectable two hours and twenty minutes later. I was also very proud of myself. The only bubbles I had consumed were water. And I enjoyed a hearty short rib steak which tasted even better knowing that it was being charged to Neil's corporate credit card.

"You look like the cat that got the cream," Mel said as she wrapped her green-nail-polished fingers over the top of our divider.

"More like the reporter who ate a hundred-dollar steak and made Neil pay for it," I said with a laugh.

She grinned evilly. "Good work, Declan. Make those arrogant assholes pay." And with an eyebrow quirk and approving nod, she slid back down into her chair and out of view.

The rest of the day flew by. Given that I had made such excellent progress on my Porter-slash-kink articles, both the official and the unofficial one, I spent the afternoon catching up on emails and ticking things off my never-ending to-do list.

Before I knew it, the same people I had watched coming into the office in the morning had started to pack up and leave. I looked up at the clock on the wall and, with an emphatic head nod, decided to do something that I never did at five. I decided to join them. I quickly packed up all of my things and placed one laptop into my top drawer and hooked the other one under my arm, taking it with me.

The icing on the cake was that not only was I leaving early—at least by my standards, anyway—but I had a hot date lined up that evening with Daylesford's sexiest Dom.

CHAPTER TWENTY-FIVE

PORTER

"Well, hello—"

Declan's sweet lips collided against my mouth before I could properly greet him. I managed to grip the front door with my fingers and steady myself on my feet.

My boy's desire was as clear as the sky was blue. I felt a surge of heat rush through my chest as he sank into me.

He cupped my face in his palms as he continued to hungrily kiss me.

Somehow, we stumbled into my entrance, and I managed to kick the front door shut.

I tried to speak, but his kissing was constant and insistent. Not that I was complaining one bit.

"Are we..." His tongue swirled around in my mouth.

"...even going..." His hand landed on the front of my pants, and he gave my cock a firm squeeze.

"...to talk?" I managed to get out.

After a few more needy moans, he peeled himself off me.

"What do you want to talk about?"

I smiled, looking at his swollen, fuller-than-normal lower lip.

"How are you feeling?" I asked.

"Good."

"How was your day?"

"Good."

"What did you have for lunch?"

"Good."

I let out a laugh. "Looks like someone has a one-track mind."

I was hoping we'd have a chance to talk about our contract, and I did notice he brought his laptop over with him, so I thought he might have wanted to as well, but as I was learning, Declan clearly wasn't in the mood for talking. Which was fine with me. There was no rush to talk about the contract stuff. I trusted him and knew we had all the time in the world to delve into that part of our relationship. We were still at beginner level, after all.

"Let's get you upstairs," I said as I brushed a wavy strand of hair from his forehead.

"Good," he said as he flung his laptop bag over his shoulder and placed it on the ground. Then his face went ghost-white.

"What's wrong?" I asked.

"Shit, I've taken the wrong laptop. This is my work one. I've left my personal one in my office."

"Is it safe?"

He chewed down on his lower lip. "Yeah, it should be. I've left it there overnight before, and nothing's ever happened. The office is secure."

"Well, then, there's nothing to worry about, is there?"

His eyes filled with worry for a moment longer until he looked at me, and then the concern was replaced with hunger. A deep, ravishing hunger.

"Take me, Porter," he said as I whisked him into my arms and took him upstairs.

We reached my bedroom. "I want to do everything we did last time," Declan said as his gaze met mine. His lips closed on the lobe of my ear. "But this time, I also want you to fuck me, Porter."

I heard each of his breaths and the noises of his mouth as he sucked on my flesh. "I was hoping you'd say that."

Normally, I liked taking my time with Declan. Part of it was because I wanted to enjoy every single second I had with him, but the real reason was that I was afraid. I didn't want to hurt him in any way, and while I had absolutely no problem with his condition, it did make me a lot more aware of all the ways that doing even seemingly normal things could cause him discomfort.

When I bought the spreader bar, I didn't know which way it would go. It could have been painful for him—and if it had been, I would have stopped straightaway and thrown the damn thing into the trash—or he could have loved it as much as he did. It warmed my heart, and stirred my cock, that he had asked for it again.

I kissed into him as urgently as his hands were exploring my body. In no time, I had his wrists tied to the edges of my bed and his feet attached to the spreader bar—exactly as requested, just like last time.

And as much as the urge to explore his body rose up within me, the memory of doing it to him before making me achingly hard, I knew I had to give my boy what he wanted.

I tore off the condom wrapper and sheathed it over my cock. I smeared a decent amount of lube over it, smoothing it out with my fingers. With the excess slick, I found his hole and delicately lubed him up.

"Are you ready, boy?"

He nodded with such force I thought his head might snap off. "Yes. Please. Sir."

There it was, that word again. Sir. And fuck if it didn't send a piercing hot vibration throughout my entire body. How was he able to do this to me, get me into such an aroused state *before* I had even entered him?

I placed the head of my cock against his hole and gently pushed through his tight ring of muscle. I paused, allowing him some time to get used to the feeling.

His eyes met mine. "Keep going. Please, Sir."

I flashed him a look of pure lust as I pushed myself about halfway in, before stopping briefly again. Then I thrust all the way in until I felt my tuft of pubic hair flush with his crack.

He closed his eyes as his body began to gently writhe on the bed underneath me. "Fuck me, Sir."

I did what he wanted, starting slowly at first. The sight of Declan tied to my bed, his feet in the spreader bar, along with the sensation of his tight hole taking my cock, was almost too much for me.

I picked up the pace. Our bodies found a good, steady rhythm, working together in perfect harmony. I kept my eyes on him, studying him for any slight hint of pain or discomfort, but I also started letting myself go more and more, falling into the pleasure and experiencing every little bit of it with him.

I trusted that Declan would tell me if something was wrong and use the safeword. I increased the pace even more. My balls tightened and I bucked my hips wildly as my orgasm tore through me. Declan followed a few seconds later, as I furiously fisted his cock until he shot streams of thick, white cum all over his stomach and chest.

I pulled out of my boy and began to untie him, first from the feet straps and then his wrists. Once I was done, I lay down next to him, our bodies sticky with sweat. Declan looked at me silently, his eyes giving off a warm glow like a porch light left on on a dark wintery night. He grazed his hand down my chest and across my abdomen.

A blush crept its way up his neck and settled in his cheeks. "I think I love you, Porter."

My heart flipped. "Well," I said, trying my damndest to conceal my smile, "that's a very romantic *thought*, Declan."

He picked up on my inflection straight away and let out the sweetest giggle. "I meant to say I do love you, Porter."

"Well, I love you too, Declan...I think."

My attempt at humor earned me a slap across the ass.

"Uh, if you think that's going to dissuade me from making any more bad jokes, I'm afraid to say you're sadly mistaken, Mr. Davies."

And with that, I cradled my boy in my arms as we fell into a deep, blissful sleep.

CHAPTER TWENTY-SIX

PORTER

I was on a high after spending the night with Declan. I'd never felt like that before, so swept up in emotion, arousal, and the overwhelming desire to totally dominate another person. He brought it all out in me, and it made me feel like the man I was meant to be.

I had found my place.

My purpose.

My boy.

I floated into the office and didn't even notice James's sour expression. It wasn't until I heard him announce, "You're early," in a way that made it clear he wasn't saying it in a *and it's great to see that you're in the office so early* kind of way, that I managed to jolt myself back into some semblance of normality.

My pulse quickened as I eyed my assistant with an equal measure of alertness and suspicion.

"I have a lot going on." I stopped when I reached his desk.

"Why are you looking at me like I just told you that Lady Gaga and Madonna are actually the same person?"

James tipped his head at my office. "He's in there."

"Who is?"

"Mayor Roberts."

"Why?"

"I take it you haven't looked at the newspapers this morning?"

"No."

A look of terror filled his eyes. "It's bad, Porter. It's really, really, bad."

I decided I'd had enough of James' cryptically vague warnings. Whatever the big scandal of the day was, I knew I could handle it. I'd sure as hell had enough practice doing that recently. I stepped toward my office, my brain frantically running over a myriad of disaster scenarios as I walked, trying to prepare myself for whatever lay in store for me.

As I opened the door, I silently prayed that Mayor Roberts wasn't embroiled in some sex scandal. That would have probably been the only situation we couldn't handle right at that moment, given everything that had happened with Mayor Smith. I took a deep breath, steadied myself, and stepped into my office.

"Mayor Roberts," I said with a spritely smile, hoping my over-enthusiasm would quell my nerves somewhat.

He was standing by the window, looking out, his back to the room. He didn't turn to acknowledge me as I entered. "What brings you by?" I kept trying to inject normality into my voice, though that was getting harder and harder to do with each word.

I placed my briefcase on my desk, and that's when I saw it. The front page of *The Daylesford Times*.

My chest tightened. It's never a good thing to see your face splashed across the front cover of the newspaper. But it was the accompanying headline that made me feel like somebody had just ripped my heart out of my chest.

Three words.

That was all it took to bring my entire world crashing down around me.

Three words.

Everything I had worked so hard for, sacrificed so much of myself to achieve, was blown up into tiny shreds.

Three fucking words.

Porter Jones Exposed.

Mayor Roberts turned around, his face twisted with anger and disappointment. "Is it true?"

I quickly scanned the articles, my eyes flying over words that leaped straight off the page and stabbed me right in the back.

Active part of Daylesford's kink community

Member of BDSM club Revolver

Reputation for sleeping around

A Dominant

Shame filled my insides. I slumped into my chair and dragged my fingers across my face. I blinked a few times, but yep, it was still there. It hadn't somehow magically disappeared. I was *The Daylesford Times'* top story of the day.

My life was over.

"Porter." The mayor's angry voice snapped me out of the pool of thoughts I was struggling to keep my head above.

I stared at the man blankly.

"Is this true?" he repeated.

"Yes," I said, hopelessly. "It appears to be true. I am involved in the kink lifestyle."

"Jesus fucking Christ." He spat the words at me.

I closed my eyes, my head was spinning. It was as if time had slowed and yet sped up at the same time. Everything was happening so fast and all at once.

A million questions raced through my mind. How could this happen? What would the fallout be? Was there any way to recover from this? And ringing louder above all of the noise was this one simple question: who did this?

I reached for the paper, my heavy fingers scraping along my desk to reach it. I picked it up and dragged it back toward me.

My mouth was so dry I could barely swallow. I prayed. I silently prayed so hard it wasn't him. That it would be any other name in the world but his. It would still be bad—nothing could change that—but it wouldn't be *rip your heart out of your chest,* nuclear-level bad.

With one eye, I peered down at the byline.

Fuck.

My stomach dropped to the floor.

There it was, in black and white.

Declan Davies.

"You're finished. You realize that, don't you?" the mayor yelled at me.

"Get out," I yelled back.

Rock bottom was bad enough without a witness like him.

"You fucking deviant." And with that, he marched out of my office, slamming the door shut loudly behind him.

I stared at the front page in disbelief. The headline, the image they had used of me from an official event from a few weeks ago— smiling as I announced a new citywide initiative to reduce litter— and then my eyes latched onto the byline and froze.

Declan. How the fuck could he do this to me?

After everything I had shared with him. I had opened up to him in ways I hadn't ever done with anyone else in my entire life. And he told me he wouldn't expose me. I remembered his words as I reached for my cell phone. The look on his face as he assured me that the article about me would be a puff piece. The hurt in his voice when he pointed out the obvious hypocrisy in exposing the mayor and not me. Was it all just a lie to lure me into a false sense of security?

The screen was lit up with dozens of missed calls, emails, and texts. I ignored them all, even the ones from Stirling, Steel, and Hudson. As much as I knew they wanted to make sure I was okay, right now, there was something else I had to do. Once I'd done it, then I'd fall into the arms of my friends and break down. But first...

I dialed the number, my fingers shaking with fury, betrayal, and hurt. So much hurt. He picked it up after just a few rings.

"Hey, baby." His voice was groggy.

"How could you do this?"

"Porter? What—what's the matter?"

"Don't play dumb with me, Declan. I'm looking at the story you wrote right now."

I heard a "shit" and what sounded like him scrambling in bed. "Wait, which story?"

What the hell did he mean by that? No, I wasn't going to get drawn into any of his bullshit.

"I want you to get out of my bed," I said, containing the rage that was threatening to escape from me. I knew that once it did, there would be no way to rein it in.

"I want you to get out of my house." The pain clenched my heart more and more with each word.

"And I want you, Declan, to get out of my life. You have betrayed me, and I never want to see you again."

I hung up and came *this close* to hurling the phone against the wall. I stood up and paced around my office, biting down on my knuckle, trying to suppress the anger I was feeling. How the fuck could he have done this to me?

I reached the wall and slammed my fist through it. The pain in my hand and wrist was immediate as my skin broke and blood trickled its way out.

I fell onto the floor, nursing my swelling hand and doing everything I could to remember how to do the simplest of things: breathe.

I slowed my breathing down as much as I could, but the firestorm of emotions I was wrapped up in wouldn't release me. Whatever reprieve I could muster would only be temporary.

I was done.

My life was over.

Declan Davies had destroyed me.

CHAPTER TWENTY-SEVEN

DECLAN

I made it from Porter's house to the office in under fifteen minutes. Given that it was a thirteen-minute Uber drive, that was no mean feat.

I ran to my desk, fueled by nerves, panic, and a spiraling sense that the tectonic plates of my life were shifting and would leave it changed forever. I felt people's stares on me and their hushed whispers as I raced past them to my cubicle.

The second I reached it and dropped my backpack on the floor, Mel was by my side a nanosecond later. "Declan, oh my god, congratulations." She was beaming at me, oozing with pride and happiness for what she must have thought was my third consecutive scoop. But I wasn't happy. I was furious, and scared that my worst fears were about to be realized.

Ignoring her, I reached for the top drawer under my desk and pulled it open forcefully. I stared down. It was empty, my laptop was gone. Someone had taken it.

"Declan, what's wrong?" Mel asked, looking into the empty drawer.

I saw her two perfectly manicured eyebrows pulled together tightly, worry etched across her, as always, perfectly made-up face.

"That article I wrote wasn't for *The Daylesford Times*, Mel," I whispered loudly into her ear.

She scrunched up her nose at me. "I don't understand, Declan."

"I also write for a whole bunch of other blogs and online sites using different names. That article was for a kink site. And it wasn't finished. I hadn't had a chance to anonymize yet."

"Oh." She took a half-step back as she processed what I was telling her. "So, how did that article end up on the front page?"

"My laptop. I accidentally left my personal laptop here and took my work one home instead yesterday." I pointed at the empty drawer as my body flooded with sadness and defeat. "Someone took it, and they published the story that was on my personal laptop."

Mel's blue eyes turned icy. "Who the fuck would do that?"

That's when it hit me. There was only one person in the office that would be this low, this vindictive to do what I was sure he had done. I shook my head. "Un-be-lievable."

"Declan, where are you going?" Mel cried after me as I stormed across the floor and to the elevator.

Once inside, my fingers smashed the button for the top floor. "That slimy, greasy-faced fucker," I said to myself, grateful there was no one in there with me. My fingers clenched into fists, and I burst out angrily onto the floor the second the doors opened.

I marched over to Neil's corner office and barged right on in. He was talking on the phone, but that didn't stop his lips from curling into a snide smile as I slammed my hands on his desk.

He hung up. "Can I help you, Declan?"

"You can start by wiping your face," I said. "You've got more oil on it than a turkey glaze."

"That's a little petty now, isn't it, Declan?" He got to his feet and looked at me like I was nothing.

But I wouldn't let him make me feel like I was useless, or stupid, or whatever else it was that he was trying to make me feel.

My hands *were* trembling, and my voice *was* shaky, but it was because I was boiling with pent-up rage, not because I was scared or intimidated. Not even for a second.

"I want my laptop back," I snarled.

"Declan, I don't know what you're—"

Before he could finish whatever bullshit he was about to sprout, I walked around his desk and lunged for his drawers.

"Okay, okay, okay," he said, pushing me aside. Pain simmered in my right side, but with the way I was feeling, it barely registered. He leaned over and opened a desk drawer. He took out my laptop bag and handed it to me.

I snatched it from him, checking it quickly to make sure my laptop was in fact in there.

"You know," he chortled. "You should actually be thanking me. I did you a favor."

"Are you fucking kidding me?" In addition to being a stealing slimeball of shit, was the man also delusional?

"I got you your third big story of the year, Declan." He said it with a smugness that, for the first time in my life, actually made me want to punch another person in the face.

"I didn't even put my name on it. And believe me, I should have. It was a mess when I read it. I cleaned it up nicely for you, Declan."

"You had no right to take my laptop or to touch my article." My jaw was clenched so tightly I was amazed I could get the words out.

"Oh god, it's true. You do like him." The sneering judgment in his tone was unmistakable. But I didn't care what he thought. He couldn't make me feel bad for liking—no, wait, loving who I loved.

"Well, at least now you know that your little boyfriend or whatever he is to you," he waved at the words he was speaking as if he was grossed out just by saying them, "is a filthy pervert."

Silence. The only sound in the room was his pathetic,

wheezing chest pushing air in and out of his mouth. Our mini-stare-off would have gone on for a lot longer, but his thin lips stretched as a light bulb went off inside of him.

"Holy shit," he said with a half-laugh. "You know what he's into. And...and you still like him?"

I didn't know what to say. I knew what I wanted to do. I wanted to defiantly tell him that he could take his smallminded, bigoted opinions and shove them up his ass. I wanted to stand up for myself and say, with pride and no sense of embarrassment, guilt or shame, that I was a submissive boy.

But I didn't.

I couldn't.

Because the truth was part of his judgment had pierced into me.

"I—I..." My stammering didn't help.

His eyes filled with disgust. "This whole kink thing is so wrong. It's depraved. You can't possibly be into it?"

"And what if I am?" I shot back without thinking, regretting it immediately. That was not the way I wanted him to find out about me. It was too defensive. It was so powerless, but it was too late. I couldn't rewind time and have a do-over.

"I don't even want to look at you anymore. Take your laptop and get the fuck out of my office. You disgust me."

His words thundered in my head as I turned around and walked out of his office. I tried to make sense of the torrent of thoughts racing through me, but I couldn't. There were too many, and the current was too strong.

I had ruined Porter's career. He would never forgive me for it.

I hadn't been able to stand up for myself in front of slimy-faced Neil.

I was a coward. A hypocrite. A totally unfuckable freak.

My head fell under the current, and I was being pulled further and further down.

I was drowning.

CHAPTER TWENTY-EIGHT

PORTER

"Thanks for letting me stay here, Steel," I said as the sounds of four beer cans being opened fizzed around me.

He shot me a sympathetic look. "Hey, of course, Porter. I'm just glad I could do something to help out."

The paparazzi had been camped outside my house ever since the story had broken two days ago. Luckily for me, one of my best friends lived in a penthouse, which was about as paparazzi-free as you could get. Although the doorman had told Steel that a couple of them had tried to sneak in through the lower ground floor entrance.

I looked across at my three closest friends, and the glum expressions on their faces said it all. I was up shit creek without a paddle. Heck, I didn't even have a kayak.

The boys—Mikey, Nick, and Liam—had gone out for dinner at Betty's, but I really knew that they did it to give us some time alone. I appreciated their friendly gesture as the four of us sat in

Steel's living room, debriefing and drinking. Not necessarily in that order.

Although no amount of drinking could numb me to the pain of Declan's betrayal.

"How could he have done this to me?" I asked the group for what was probably the hundredth time that evening.

"Have you spoken to him?" Hudson's gentle voice, as always, felt so reassuring.

"Does yelling count?" I answered, half-jokingly.

It was my first weak attempt at humor in days, but there was nothing funny about how I had been feeling. I couldn't believe that the first person I had ever opened up to, and let in so close to my heart and my deepest desires, could turn around and do something like this to me. The initial shock had left me, and I was left wallowing in a dark, cold, and heavy pit of shame, hurt, and downright despair.

"What are you going to do...professionally, that is?" Steel, ever the pragmatist, asked, moving the conversation on slightly.

"What *can* I do?" I replied with a sulky resignation as I took a swig of beer.

"Is there any way you could maneuver, or strategize, or wave the magic wand that you have to fix this?" Stirling forced a smile and lifted his eyes at me, as if he was willing himself, as much as me, to believe that somehow there was a way out of this mess.

But there wasn't, and we all knew it. And that was the worst fucking feeling in the world.

I dragged my fingers through my hair. "Nope," I said dejectedly. "There is no way out here, guys. No amount of spin can undo the damage that's been done."

"Well, hang on a minute there," Hudson said, reaching over and placing his hand supportively on my forearm. "Liam and I have been traveling all around the country, even to places where his message hasn't traditionally been accepted."

He took a sip of his beer before continuing. "And sure, people aren't always receptive to receiving a message they don't like. I've seen that up close and personal for myself. Some people are determined to dig their heels in and pretend that things like climate change aren't real. Liam calls those kinds of people *the unchangeables.*"

"It's a little more diplomatic than *deplorables,*" Steel joked, and we all chuckled.

"No matter what you say to these people, no matter how much evidence you present to them, absolutely nothing will get them to change their minds. They're stuck in their ways of thinking, and for whatever reason, they're happy with that."

"So, how does that help *me?*" I sent a quizzical look Hudson's way.

"Well, the good news for you, my friend, is that for every one *unchangeable,* there are at least two or three people who *are* willing to listen and consider different or new perspectives. And it's those people that you want to reach, because they're the ones who are open to it."

We drank in silence for a moment. I turned Hudson's words over in my mind. Was it even remotely possible to dig myself out of this hole? Were there enough people in Daylesford who would be open to it—or at least be able to look past it—to allow me to continue in my career?

A tiny glimmer of possibility rose in my chest, but I quickly pushed it back down. I knew better than to get my hopes up. I'd been in the political game long enough to know that this story didn't have a happy ending, no matter how much I wanted to believe otherwise. If a pegging piece led the mayor to resign, the mayor's chief of staff being exposed as a Dom could only lead to the same outcome.

"Daylesford's a pretty progressive city, Porter," Stirling said, doing his best to send me an optimistic smile. "Maybe people could be open to the idea of a Dom mayor?"

I wanted to believe it but couldn't help but scoff at the idea.

"Yeah, maybe in fifty years, Stirling. But not in the 2020s. This is way too soon. The world, I'm sorry to say, just isn't ready."

We all slumped a little further into our seats as we fell into a depressed silence. The reality was that my career was over. Just like Mayor Smith before me, I wouldn't be able to get out of this alive. I would have to resign.

"What day is it?" I asked.

"Tuesday," Steel answered.

God, it felt like Friday.

"Why?" he asked, his light blue eyes meeting mine.

I shrugged. "No reason."

I would be lucky to see the week out.

My phone buzzed in my pants pocket. I took it out, and my eyes widened. I stared down at the screen, unable to convince myself that what I was looking at was real and not a figment of my imagination.

I looked up at my friends, my mouth gaping wide open, but no words were coming out. I was speechless.

What on earth had Declan done now?

CHAPTER TWENTY-NINE

DECLAN

I took a deep breath in, my mouse hovering over the button. If I did this, if I pressed *Send*, it would change my life forever.

But hey, my life was turbo-fucked at the moment, so at least it couldn't get any worse, right?

I thought.

I hoped.

I propped myself up a little higher in my bed and stretched my legs out in front of me. It was sad to admit, but the familiar feeling of low-level pain coursing through my lower back was actually comforting. At least it was something I could always rely on.

I glanced at the laptop I was propping up on my legs, scanning the screen, looking at the words I had typed. Actually, it felt more like they had poured out of me. Reading them back again was almost like an out-of-body experience. I remembered typing them, but I had no idea where they came from. It was me, but at the same time, I felt like someone reading them for the very first time.

I exhaled as my finger tapped the mouse. With one click, I had done it. I had submitted the story I was meant to write. It was very likely to be the last article I would ever submit to *The Daylesford Times*. There was an almost certain probability that after this, I would be not only disgraced and fired, but also blacklisted by every other respectable media organization in the country.

This wasn't some political scandal exposing the private life of a public figure. No, this time, the story was about someone that you normally never read about: The faceless name in the byline accompanying the story, never the subject of the story itself.

This article was different. It was about me. I was exposing—myself. Or at least, telling my truth.

It was the right thing to do and something I should have done a lot earlier.

I couldn't change anything that had happened. What was done was done. But if I wanted to find a way to be able to live with myself, I had to stop hiding and being such a fucking hypocrite. I always talked about telling the truth and why the truth was so important, so how could I go on avoiding my own?

It was the very least I could do.

An email notification *ping* alerted me to the fact that my article had been successfully submitted. I glanced over it again.

The headline was simple. *My Truth.*

The opening line was the hardest, most painful sentence I had ever written. But at the same time, a small bubble of pride filled my insides as I reread it to myself for the gazillionth time that night.

I've decided to grow a backbone, which, coming from a submissive boy with scoliosis, is a bad joke—but one that I'm allowed to make. Although there's nothing funny about what I have to say. I'm writing this article because I, Declan Davies, need to be honest about who I am.

· · ·

Never in my wildest dreams did I imagine I would be writing an article like this.

With kink as the subject matter.

About myself.

And submitted to a mainstream organization that I worked for, using my real name.

No hiding behind a thin veil of anonymity. Nope, I was putting myself front and center.

The timing was far from ideal, given everything that was happening with Porter, but maybe, in a way, it actually made it the right time to do it.

Even though the two mayoral stories were a big break for me and got me a lot of buzz and attention, they never sat right with me. First, there was the slightly shady way I had obtained the information. Even though the hacker I worked with claimed to be ethical, it was still a dubious ethical area.

But more importantly, I never disclosed that I had a vested interest in the story, due to being both a submissive boy and the mayor's illegitimate son. That last part I left out intentionally, knowing full well that if I revealed it, *that* would become the story. Mom had already gone through enough pain, I didn't want to subject her to it again.

But being a submissive boy? That part I probably should have mentioned. I didn't though, and I convinced myself the reason to not disclose it was because the story wasn't about me. I wasn't the public figure, the mayor was.

But by not being upfront about that part, I was doing something worse than breaking a reporting convention: I was throwing a fellow member of the kink community under the bus. Well and truly. If I was applying one standard to him, I should have applied the same standard to myself. It was the only right thing to do.

I let out a loud yawn. It was only ten, so still relatively early, but I hadn't slept a wink since the Porter story broke. But before I could go to sleep, I knew I had one more thing to do that night.

I reached over and grabbed my phone from my night stand. My chest tightened, gripped with a fear even bigger than what I had felt submitting the actual article.

It was the only thing left I could do.

I tapped away furiously, and when I was done, clicked on the green button. With that, I'd sent Porter a text with a copy of the article I had just written.

I let out another deep breath. Whatever happened next, only one thing was certain: my life would never be the same again.

CHAPTER THIRTY

PORTER

I finally popped my head out of my shame hole, leaving Steel's penthouse before the sun had even risen and sneaking into the office at the crack of dawn on Friday. I couldn't deal with looking anyone in the face and trying to explain myself to them. My entire carefully constructed life had just been exposed for the entire world to see—and it was not a world that would understand, much less accept me.

I had been working from home since the story broke, under the guise of not feeling well. That part was true. I felt like absolute shit. But that cover story was only a thinly veiled mask hiding the real reason why I was keeping a low profile—and why I was seriously considering selling up and moving out of town—as my body, mind, and soul were rocked by an unrelentless tide of shame and horror that kept sweeping through me.

Everyone in the whole city—hell, anyone with an internet connection—knew. They all had front-row seats to the most intimate, private parts of my life. How could I live with that? Everywhere I would go, there would be looks and whispers of judgment...or worse. I had stayed off social media entirely, but I was sure that commentators and trolls alike were having a field day with this story.

I thought back to the level of vitriol Mayor Smith had experienced when the pegging story broke. This felt a thousand times worse. This *was* a thousand times worse.

I picked up an empty box, took it over to the bookcase behind my desk, and began filling it up quickly, not necessarily carefully. I didn't want to spend any more time in the office than I had to. Ideally, I wanted to be out of there by the time James got in, which was usually around seven-thirty.

I heard footsteps outside. I walked over to the small window looking out into the reception area and sighed heavily. Of course today had to be the day that James decided to show up just after six. Could nothing go right for me at all?

I lunged at the light switch by the door and flicked it off. Maybe he hadn't seen that I was in? I had Ubered in to work, so my parking spot was empty. I tiptoed back across to the bookcase and continued packing, just as quickly, and as quietly as I could, hoping I could evade James for a little while longer.

There was an unnecessary knock on the door before it swung wide open.

"Porter Jones." James said my name with so much enthusiasm it sounded like he was announcing I had won the lottery.

"Hey, James." I glanced at him briefly. I didn't want to be rude, but I didn't want to look into his eyes either. I couldn't. I wasn't ready yet. It would be too devastating. Even though we were close and he was in the lifestyle, too, I just couldn't bring myself to properly look at him.

Out of the corner of my eye, I saw him bouncing into the room. He placed a copy of what I assumed was *The Daylesford Times* on my desk before sitting himself down. I looked over at him, holding my gaze a little longer this time. His lips were stretched in the widest smile I had ever seen on him.

What the hell was going on? Why was he sounding—and looking—like my whole world hadn't just ended?

I couldn't help it. My curiosity got the better of me. I placed the books that were in my hand into the box and walked over to my desk, eyeing him suspiciously as I did. Something was definitely going on and I wanted to know what it was. I glanced down at the newspaper and almost fell head over feet.

I was shocked. It couldn't have been real. It made no sense. I flicked the newspaper in my hands, as if the ink would magically transform into a headline that actually made sense.

I looked over at James, my forehead a mass of wrinkled confusion. This couldn't be real. He must have gone to one of those printing places where people go and order a custom-made humorous front page to put up in their basements or man caves. There was no way what I was looking at was legit. It absolutely, one hundred percent couldn't be.

"Is this a joke?" I stared up at him.

He shook his head and raised his hands in the air. "This is no joke, Porter. What you're looking at there is today's front page of *The Daylesford Times.*"

I turned my attention back to the newspaper and began reading the article, determined to confirm if it was, in fact, real. I still wasn't convinced. I scanned the first few lines. Okay, it seemed real enough. But I still had no fucking clue what was going on.

"I assume you haven't been online much these last few days?" James guessed.

I scratched the back of my neck. "That would be hard *no*. I've been avoiding the internet—and social media especially—like the modern plague on humanity that it is."

James' lips curled upward into a soft smile. "Ah, that explains it."

"Explains what? Can you please tell me what the hell is going on, James? I just want to pack my shit up and get out of here before I have to face everybody else in the office. It's hard enough just looking at you."

"Gee, thanks, boss," he said, but I could hear the humor in his voice.

"I'm sorry. I didn't mean it like that, James. I'm just... I'm just... I don't know what I am, frankly. Apart from mortified that I've been so publicly humiliated and devastated that everything I've worked my entire life for is completely ruined."

"I know what you're going through," James started, before he corrected himself. "I mean, I can only imagine what you're going through, Porter. And I feel for you. Believe me, with every fiber of my being, I feel so bad about what you are experiencing." As a fellow kinkster, his heartfelt genuineness was actually a little comforting.

"But you, Porter Jones, can stop packing your shit up, because you are not going anywhere. Unless, of course, you've suddenly decided that you don't want to be Daylesford's next mayor."

My brain did that funny thing where it registered the words it had heard, but it couldn't even begin to process them. What on earth was James talking about? My chief of staff career was over, much less any shot I had at the top job. I was still just as confused as before.

He must have seen it on my face and let out a quiet giggle. "Sit down and I'll fill you in."

I walked over to my chair and sat down on the edge of it. "Short version please. Start near the end."

He grinned. "So, here's the deal. Declan published yet another story this week. It went live late on Tuesday."

"Yeah, I know," I interrupted. "He sent it to me as well."

"Right, that's great. So, you would have read that it was a brilliantly insightful piece about the kink community and all of the double standards and bullshit that still exists in the world when it comes to judging our lifestyle?"

I nodded. "Yeah, it was pretty good. So?"

"So...it went mega-viral. His piece got picked up by every major outlet in the *world*, Porter. This has gone international."

"Fuck," I exclaimed. I was so confused, I had no idea what to make of all of this. "And that's a good thing?"

James flashed me a look that screamed *fuck yeah* loud and clear.

"I have no idea how these viral things work and what makes something so popular," he began. "Maybe it was because he opened up about his scoliosis and really went there, but this article has been, like, universally lauded. Sure, there's maybe a handful of asshole trolls, but the response has been like ninety-nine percent positive."

"That's unheard of, James. That—that never happens."

James nodded emphatically and widened his eyes. "Exactly! The story has been everywhere this week, and so I'm not surprised that *this* has happened." He tilted his head toward the newspaper sitting on my desk.

I looked down again at the headline, and slowly, it began to make a little more sense.

99 Daylesford Citizens Come Out as Kinky

"How—how did this happen?" I asked James.

His eyes were soft and kind. "Declan's story really moved people, Porter. It was such a brave, ballsy thing to do, coming out as a submissive boy to the entire world like he did. I guess it inspired other people to follow him and do the same."

I clapped my hand against my face, still in a state of shock. "Wow." It was all I could manage.

"Wow, indeed. I've read the article, not in full detail, but I did quickly skim through it. And a lot of Daylesford's biggest names are in it," James said.

"Really? Like who?"

"Yep," James replied as he leaned over my desk and reached for the paper. He picked it up. "You've got the dean of the university who is into pup play. You've got a lawyer—I can't remember his name—who is into being tied up and gagged. Mr. Redman, one of Daylesford's richest men and our biggest donor, is into crossdressing, and there's even a poly housewife in there into whipping her husband—and their two girlfriends."

"Holy crap." I was still finding it hard to find words for what I was thinking. This was unbelievable.

Firstly, there was Declan's courage to write his story and share it with the world like he had. For a guy who was almost too scared to take his shirt off and jump into my pool, that was freaking huge. I knew how uncomfortable he still was about his body, and when it came to boundaries between work life and sex life, he was almost as strict about it as I had been. He hadn't told anyone in his life that he was a submissive, not even his best friend.

And then there was the reaction from the people of Daylesford themselves, choosing to out themselves as proud members of the kink lifestyle—something that was fraught with huge amounts of danger and risk for some of them, including losing their jobs and being ostracized by friends and family—as a sign of their solidarity with me. It was beyond anything I could have ever dreamed.

"So," James said, getting to his feet. "Barring some major fuckup, and if the people of Daylesford vote consistently with what the polls are telling us, you, Porter Jones, will be Daylesford's next mayor."

He walked over to the door, but before he let himself out, he looked over his shoulder and gave a knowing smile. "And Daylesford's first Dom mayor."

I fell back into my chair, rocking slightly, as a lifetime of pent-up emotions whirled throughout my body. I still couldn't quite comprehend the enormity of what was happening.

I could be out.

Open.

Myself.

My truest self.

That thought had never entered my mind before as an even

remotely practical possibility. It would have been like telling people in the 1950s that, one day, same-sex marriage would be the law of the land. It just seemed so beyond reach. A hope for another generation, but little more than a fantasy in my own lifetime.

But now all of that had been blown apart. The world had experienced a seismic shift, opening up a future for me that I didn't think would ever exist.

And it was all because of one person.

I reached for my phone and hurriedly sent out a text. I looked around my office. Packing was the last thing I felt like doing, especially now that there was a chance it would be completely unnecessary.

I grabbed my phone, keys, and jacket and ran out of the office and past one completely shocked assistant. "Porter, where are you—?"

I was out of there so fast that I didn't even hear the rest of James' question.

I was on my way to see the bravest, most beautiful boy in the world. And nothing was going to slow me down or get in my way.

CHAPTER THIRTY-ONE

DECLAN

One foot in front of the other. That's what I kept reminding myself as I walked up the beautifully landscaped and meticulously maintained front yard of Porter's house.

My heart had been thundering in my chest since the second I had received his text—he wanted to see me at his place within the hour. That was all it said. That was all he needed to say.

I just wanted to see him one more time. Even if he wanted to yell at me, which he had every right to do, I was determined to do anything—even getting down on my hands and knees—to beg the man for a chance to explain my side of the story. After that, whatever happened next, I would have to find a way to be okay with it.

I just needed to let him know that even though it wasn't my fault, that it wasn't me who published the story about him, I took full responsibility for it, and I was so, so, *so* sorry for the pain I had caused him and the damage I had done to his career.

My pulse quickened as I approached the massive, wood-paneled front door. I stood there staring blankly at it, my stomach knotted with nerves. It felt like it was going to take all of my energy to raise my hand and knock. Just as I started to move, the door flung wide open.

And there he stood. My breath hitched in my throat at the sight of him. It was as if my brain had momentarily forgotten just how stunningly attractive the man was. Even in something as simple as jeans and a grey shirt, he still managed to take my breath away. Literally.

I tripped over my feet, falling against the door frame and struggling to breathe. His strong arms caressed my body as he gently pulled me up. I swallowed as our eyes met.

Just as I was starting to find my feet again, he flashed me a friendly grin. My legs turned to jelly. "Come in, let's sit you down." There was a light authority in his voice that tugged at something inside of me. It was the tiniest sliver of desire...and hope.

He carefully walked me into his living room, and we sat down together on the couch. "Let me get you some water."

"No, Porter, you don't have to—"

The look he shot me as he whipped his head in my direction stopped me mid-sentence. It sent a spark of electricity through my entire body. I knew that look. I liked that look. I would spend the rest of my life crawling on my hands and knees just to have that look directed at me over and over again.

Was it possible?

He returned a few moments later with a full glass of water which I proceeded to drain. It wasn't until I placed the empty glass on the coffee table that I realized just how much I needed it. I flashed him a look of gratitude, and he smiled.

Yes, *that* smile. That dorky, uneven, and totally fucking adorable smile. My insides melted and I wanted nothing more than to leap across the couch and press my body into his. I just needed to touch him, smell him, and feel his hands all over my body. My senses were aroused, and I could tell he knew just by looking at me.

But no, first we had to talk.

And so I did.

It all spilled out of me. How I was writing two articles, one which intended for *The Daylesford Times* and the other for *Connect Kink*. How Neil was the biggest jerk in the history of jerks and had stolen my laptop and published the wrong article to the wrong website. And how soul-deep sorry I was that by being so stupid and leaving my personal laptop at work, I had single-handedly ruined his entire career.

By the time I was done talking, I felt like I had run a marathon. All of my energy was gone. I stared down at my hands in my lap, unable to bring myself to look at him. Even though I was dying to know what he was thinking, the thought of him being angry at me, of him hating me, was too much to bear.

After silence—way too much silence—I decided to tip my head up. He was staring at me, but his eyes were soft and kind. "Come here," he said softly as he extended his hand toward me.

I grabbed it in a heartbeat and allowed myself to be pulled into him in one smooth, solid movement. Our lips fused together as the warmth of his body pressed into mine, sending tingles across my skin.

He tasted and felt as good as I remembered. Better, even. I felt a twinge of pain in my mid-back, but I ignored it, kissing him deeper. It was all I wanted to do: be lost in this kiss with him, forever. Everything else in the world could fall away. I only wanted this.

"Wait." I struggled to unmesh my lips from his, but I knew I had to. "You're not angry at me?"

A heavy look flashed across his face. "I'm not going to lie to you. I was, Declan. I was furious with you at the start of the week when the article came out. It—it destroyed me."

The pain in his voice felt like ten thousand arrows stabbing my heart.

"I cannot tell you how sorry I am," I said, wishing there were words invented that were better at expressing how I was feeling. Those didn't come anywhere near close enough.

"I know you are. I believe you. Even when I didn't know what happened and I had to assume that it was you that had published the story about me, there was a part of me that never stopped believing in you, Declan. I thought... I thought—"

His voice cracked. "I thought it was just wishful thinking, but now I know that it was true."

His arms wrapped tighter around me as I leaned in closer to him, allowing him to envelop me.

"And then the article you wrote about yourself and kink... Holy shit."

I smiled and looked up at him. "You liked it?"

His jaw clenched. "No."

My breath caught in my throat.

His eyes narrowed in on me. "I loved it."

Breathing out the biggest sigh of relief, I playfully slapped him across the chest. "Porter, you had me there for a second. Geez."

"What you did took guts, Declan. You risked everything, because even though it's great that it got the amazing reception that it has, it could have also gone the other way. You could have lost your job, your friends, everything. And the whole world would have known something incredibly private and intimate about you as well."

"I know," I said, pushing that nightmare scenario out of my thoughts. I was beyond grateful that it hadn't happened. "But that was a chance I was prepared to take. I had a good reason."

Porter's light green eyes lit up in recognition. "Wait, you mean you wrote that article...for me?"

I nodded. "Yes. At least, that's how it started out. I guess I figured it was a way I could apologize to you. But then, when I started writing it, a funny thing happened."

A frown line emerged on his forehead. "And what was that?"

"I started writing it...for me." I took a few breaths, overcome by the memory of the experience. Porter gently stroked down my arm, and the reassurance felt heavenly.

"I have spent my whole life afraid of showing people who I really am. I've been embarrassed by my body, or felt like an outsider at work who didn't fit in, or felt ashamed for wanting to be submissive."

"I know the feeling," Porter said softly, and it felt good knowing that he knew exactly what I was talking about.

"I didn't want to live my life being scared anymore. My body is the way that it is."

"And it's beautiful and perfect, baby." Porter's soft lips pressed into my forehead.

"I am the way that I am at work. I'm never going to be the stereotypical image of a ruthless reporter that I have in my head, you know?"

"You don't have to be that, Declan. You're an amazing reporter in your own right, just as you are."

I gave a quick nod of recognition. "Yeah, damn straight I am."

We both laughed, and some of the tension left the room. I snuggled in closer against Porter's hard body.

"And I cannot tell you how *beyond* over it I am of being ashamed of my kink. I am a boy, and I am a sub, and I want to scream it from the mountaintops so that the whole world hears it."

"Well, I think you achieved that with your article," Porter said with a wide grin.

"Good," I said firmly, as I sat up and twisted around to face Porter straight on. The heat emanating from his body made me all gooey inside.

"Hold that thought," he said as he jumped off the couch and

disappeared out of the room. When he reappeared a few moments later, he held a piece of paper in his hand.

"What's that?" I asked, looking at it.

A smile spread across his face. "It's our contract. I've been working on a second, slightly more thorough draft."

A rush of arousal coursed through my veins as he handed it to me.

"We'll need to discuss it, and obviously I want to include all of your input, as well. It's equally important to me."

"I don't want to talk right now, Porter." My words dripped with need.

"Later then?" He raised both eyebrows at me.

"Later," I agreed. "But right now, take me upstairs, tie me up, and fuck me."

EPILOGUE 1

Six months later...

DECLAN

"What about this one?" I placed the pale blue business shirt, still hanging on the clothes hanger, in front of my chest and turned to Porter.

"Hmm." His fingers scrubbed his chin as he tilted his head to the side, taking me in. "Show me the other one again."

I rolled my eyes. This was getting ridiculous. I had pretty much shown him every single tailor-made business shirt that I now owned, and he still couldn't tell me which one I should wear. I threw the light blue shirt on the bed and stepped over to the closet to pick out another one.

"There, that's the one," Porter said with a loud enthusiasm.

"Uh, Porter," I said with a half-smile. "I'm not even wearing anything yet." I was wearing a pair of black pants, but despite spending the last ten minutes trying on shirts, I was still very much shirtless.

"I know." The low tone in his voice stirred my cock.

"You're being terrible, Porter," I said with a giggle. "I can't exactly leave the house without a shirt, now can I?"

"Why not?" Porter replied, feigning seriousness. "I certainly wouldn't object."

"I'm going to go with the white shirt," I said, pulling it off the clothes hanger for the third time that morning.

"Oh, are you now?" Porter had crept up behind me, and his fingers had wrapped themselves around my waist. His touch sent a reassuring warmth across my skin.

My eyes widened, and I turned around to face him. "I mean, if you will let me, Sir."

I looked into his eyes and noticed the little spark that filled them every time I called him that. He loved it—almost as much as I did.

"Actually, my boy," he said as he played with a loose strand of hair that had fallen over my ear. "Our contract expired yesterday."

"Oh, time to renew, then?" I said with a hopeful smile.

His face grew serious. "Yes, it is, Declan."

"Same as always?"

After spending about a month discussing what we both wanted from our relationship, as well as our preferences in the bedroom, Porter and I had spent the past five months in a contract. Well, actually, in a series of contracts.

Since we were both new to this, we decided to take a slower approach. Our first contract was just for a weekend. After that, we sat down and talked about what we wanted to do next.

The next few contracts were for a period of a week. And again, after each contract had ended, we discussed it to make sure that we were both happy with everything, and made any adjustments that were needed, before moving on to the next contract.

For the last three months, we had switched to monthly contracts. After our last contract ended, we decided that we had gotten the formula just right and that no changes were needed for the next contract. I assumed this month's contract extension would be merely a formality.

"Why don't you get changed and I'll get started on breakfast, hey?" Porter said as he pressed his lips to my forehead.

"Uh, okay. Sure."

"Great, I'll see you downstairs."

And with that, he was off, leaving me to finish getting dressed. I sensed that he wanted to talk about something, but I wasn't worried. That was probably the biggest change I had experienced in my life over the last six months: I had developed an inner confidence and strength that I had never felt before.

To say that releasing the kink article about myself changed my life would have been a massive understatement. There was my life before that article, and then there was my life after it.

Before the article, I was a scared little boy who didn't know who he was, and in all honesty, was afraid to find out. I cared so much about what people thought about me that I had overlooked getting to know who I actually was first.

I felt like an outsider. A fake. Someone who didn't deserve to be happy because there was always something I could find fault with about myself. My body was broken. I wasn't driven enough to be a successful reporter. I wasn't rich and successful enough to have an amazing boyfriend. I didn't deserve to find my perfect Dom.

But the overwhelming love and acceptance that I received after the article was published shattered everything I ever thought about myself. It made me question all of my self-limiting beliefs, and it forced me to challenge myself and push through them.

It wasn't always easy, and I didn't get things right every single time, but I didn't feel broken anymore. Or stupid. Or unlovable. Or not damn good enough. Or any of those shitty things that used to plague my mind twenty-four-seven.

Instead, I was living out some of the best advice I had received in my life. I focused on doing the right thing, and I used that as my anchor during some very difficult times, just like my mom had said.

That also made me happy. I was being true to who I was and what I felt inside. And in the words of Mrs. Langley, that was really all that mattered.

And like Mel suggested, I was just being me. No more putting on a show to try and play into other people's expectations of me. I was done trying to fit into some mold in order to get other people's approval or become a ruthless asshole just to get ahead.

I was a nice guy, and I was a nice reporter who wrote amazing stories. If my editors or colleagues couldn't see that, well then, that was their problem, not mine.

It also meant no more ill-fitting suits. Porter had taken care of that. It was even written into our very first contract: A shopping spree at his choice of designer boutiques. He had complete control over what I wore. Not to mention what I ate, when I went to bed, and a whole list of other things for which I had surrendered to him.

In some ways, that was my biggest hurdle to overcome. I carried so much shame and so many feelings of inferiority about how strong my submissive desires were. For years, I used to think that there was something wrong with me for wanting someone else to make all of my decisions for me. But after hearing from hundreds of submissives from all over the world who had read my article and could relate, I learned that I wasn't alone and that there was nothing wrong with me.

Choosing to give control over any aspect in your life to someone else was one of the most special, sacred things that could happen between people. I wasn't weak, and it didn't make me any lesser as a person for what I wanted. It was simply a part of me, who I was. In fact, it took a bucketload of strength to acknowledge my desires and act on them.

And that was the key difference with Porter. He wasn't using or taking advantage of me the way John had. We came into this relationship as equals, no matter what the power dynamic looked like.

I scratched my head as I looked at the white shirt again. I wasn't sure about it. Damn, *this* was why I needed a Dom to make these sorts of decisions for me. Even having to make a simple choice like what to wear left me feeling cloudy and confused.

I grabbed the white shirt and quickly put it on. I felt a twinge of pain in my lower back. Unfortunately, that hadn't changed since falling in love and being with Porter. But almost daily sessions of being tied up were the best kind of physical therapy I had ever had.

I was still buttoning the shirt up as I entered the kitchen. My mind flashed back to the first time I had come into Porter's kitchen, under very different circumstances.

"Why are you smiling like that?" Porter was putting out plates on the table when he looked up at me.

"I was just thinking about the first time I walked into this kitchen. I believe you were standing by the stove, making a delicious breakfast for me."

He licked his lips. "Is that all you remember?"

I knew exactly what he was doing, but I was happy to cave in. "You, uh, *may* not have been wearing a shirt."

"Oh yeah." He moved away from the table and closed the space between us.

"And what did you think about that?"

"Well, I was pretty hungover..."

"That you were." He gently traced his index finger over my lower lip.

"Hey, you," I said, giving him a playful slap across his chest.

He looked down, and when he looked back up at me, there was a fiery blaze in his eyes. "I will allow that minor infraction." His voice was a hushed whisper. "Since we're technically in between contracts."

"Well, thank you, Sir," I whispered back, my face flamed with heat.

"But," he said, taking a step back, "that's exactly what I would like to talk to you about, Declan. I've made breakfast." He motioned his hand at the table.

I followed him to the table and sat down. "I just made the usual," Porter said. "I didn't mean to decide for you, but we will have to get going after this."

"Thank you." I eyed the delicious-smelling bacon and eggs in front of me. "I understand, and I appreciate you doing this."

We both started eating, and after a few mouthfuls, Porter got up. He walked over to the counter and picked up a piece of paper. His face was neutral as he placed the paper on the table and slid it across.

"Is this the new contract?" I asked.

"It is." The serious look returned to his face again.

"Same as last time?"

His jaw clenched. "No."

"Oh."

His eyes lingered on me for a moment before he turned his attention to the contract I had picked up and was reading through.

"I think we're ready to move on from beginner level, Declan."

I smiled, liking what I was hearing. I was definitely ready to step things up a notch. "Uh-huh. What are you saying, Porter?"

His eyes went dark, stormy. "I'd like to make this contract...longer."

"How much longer?"

Part of me wanted to hear him say the word *forever*, but we had discussed that. As nice as that sentiment was, we agreed that we preferred shorter contracts as it gave us the option to reflect and renegotiate things as we changed as people. The idea of being locked into something fixed and long-term didn't appeal to either one of us.

"Six months." His face tightened, but he continued speaking. "I know we talked about keeping the contract terms short, and we can always have a clause that we can change it at anytime, but I would like the security, the feeling of knowing that this is more permanent."

"Uh-huh."

"I've never been the kind of guy who wanted anything more permanent. Before you, I was a bit of a..."

"Slut?" I joked cheekily.

"I prefer thinking of it as being a *Samantha*," he said with a hearty laugh.

"So what you're saying is that now you're more of a Charlotte?"

He kept laughing. "I don't think I will *ever* be a Charlotte."

"Good. I am very relieved to hear that."

The laugh slowly faded from his face as a contemplative look took over.

"I was with a lot of guys before I met you, Declan. That's no secret, and I make no apologies for it."

"And you don't need to," I added.

His face softened a little. "The thing was, I never wanted anything more with any of them. It was always just a casual, fun time. But with you, Declan...I can't imagine my life without you."

My chest swelled. "I feel the same way about you, Porter."

Our hands met in the middle of the table. "So yes, I agree to a six-month contract. And to a lifetime of six-month contracts."

"Really?"

I was surprised to hear the disbelief in his voice. "Yes, really."

"Oh, baby, you have no idea how happy that makes me."

I smiled. I think I did. If it was even a fraction of how happy he made me, then I totally knew.

"Alright, we can go over the contract details later today. We do need to get going soon, though," he said, casting his eyes over at the clock on the wall.

I looked down at my plate. "I'm almost done."

"Great, you finish up. I'm going to change this tie. I don't like it."

I nodded as he left the room. I would read the contract over later with him, but as I finished my breakfast, I couldn't help but feel like my life was finally coming together.

Work-wise, I was doing great. After my 'coming out as kinky' story got the reaction that it did, I quickly scored a promotion to become *The Daylesford Times'* newest investigative reporter, with the opportunity for occasional op-ed pieces as well.

I made a promise, which I had kept so far—and had every intention of keeping for the rest of my career—that I would never compromise myself in order to get a story ever again. Not even a little bit. It just wasn't worth it. I would always just be me. If I got the story, great. If I didn't, another one would come along soon enough.

As a juicy side bonus, greasy-faced Neil got fired for the stunt that he pulled, stealing my personal laptop and publishing the story about Porter without me knowing. His attempt to sex-shame Porter backfired spectacularly, and the editorial board of the newspaper gave him his marching orders.

Self-wise, I was doing great, too. Sure, being in love wasn't a panacea for my scoliosis or for my chronic pain, but it sure did help.

I also heard over the months from so many people who had a disability and were also into kink. It helped me put my condition into perspective, but it also made me question why I had been so bothered about it in the first place.

My body was just...different. That was simply a fact. Some people had a straight spine, others didn't. Thinking that just because my body was different made me some deformed, unfuckable monster wasn't a fact. It was an opinion. One that I no longer held.

Relationship-wise, I was beyond great. I was in a state of permanent bliss. Porter Jones was my person.

My man.

My Daddy.

And my Dom.

He was strong, caring, and everything I had ever wanted. He knew what I needed intuitively and was so open and communicative that talking to him—about anything—was the easiest thing in the world.

The only—very slight—issue concerned my family. Everything

was great with my mom, but I guess in some way, I couldn't help but be a little disappointed that my biological father, Mayor Smith, had packed up and left town without ever reaching out. But he'd never made any attempt to contact me before, so why would he start now?

I did, however, find a way to console myself. While I might not have had access to the previous mayor, I did have access to Daylesford's current mayor.

The best access in town, actually.

EPILOGUE 2

PORTER

I shuffled subtly on my feet, making sure the required ever-present smile was still plastered to my face. Even though I had been on my feet for over an hour, I couldn't show signs of anything other than sheer joy and jubilation. It was a purely ceremonial act, but a significant one nonetheless.

I looked out into the crowd and smiled as I saw the faces of all of the workers and volunteers who had done so much to make this day happen. They all looked so happy, so proud, and I couldn't deny the fact that I was too.

I was the mayor of Daylesford.

The path to the top position certainly wasn't a smooth one. But then again, where would the fun in that have been?

The turnaround my life had gone through over the last six months was nothing short of spectacular. I honestly thought my chief of staff career was over, much less any political ambitions I may have been harboring. But Declan's article single-handedly changed all of that.

Not only did it result in a tsunami of support for me personally, but it completely turned the dial on the conversation around kink in Daylesford. Sure, there would always be some people who didn't like it, or accept it, or ever be open to liking and accepting it.

The *unchangeables.*

Good thing for me, then, that the majority of the people in Daylesford were very much *changeables.*

So many more people had come out as some form of kinky since Declan's article, and by bringing kink out of the shadows and into the light, it did something funny. It normalized it. No longer was kink something that other people did over there. Suddenly, it was something that a lot of people did everywhere. At the end of the day, the realization most people had about it was this—it really didn't matter.

What people chose to do in their private lives, when it came to love and sex, was their business. No one else's. Shaming people for what they liked and who they were on a deep, intrinsic level suddenly started to feel so archaic. So 2020.

I was standing behind the speaker, who was listing off a highlight reel of my biggest professional accomplishments to the audience. At that moment, I thought of Mayor Smith. My chest tightened slightly. I still felt a little bad, and a whole lot guilty, about how he had been treated. I had reached out to him recently, hoping that he and his wife Peggy were benefiting from this newfound acceptance of kink.

But he didn't return any of my calls. Which was fair enough. I couldn't blame the guy for the way he felt. I did wish he had made an effort to at least return some of Declan's calls, but the man had never shown any interest in his son before. He wanted to live his life a particular way. Even though I didn't agree with it, a big part of being accepting meant having to accept others when they didn't act in ways that you liked or could even understand. I had to practice what I was preaching.

Today's event was my official swearing-in ceremony. Strangely, it happened a month after the election and weeks after I had assumed all the responsibilities of the job. I guess it was just a little quirk from Daylesford's history that had been kept alive for all of these years.

My heart thumped with joy at the sight of my closest friends sitting in the front row, beaming with pride. Stirling, Steel, and Hudson were my family. In all the years they had known me, they never rejected me for being who I was. They loved me, warts, kinks, oversharing, and all.

I was so happy to see them sitting beside their boys. Mikey, Nick, and Liam were three of the most beautiful, sweet, sometimes sassy, always goodhearted boys you could ever hope to meet. They made their Daddies so happy, and that thought made me feel like my chest would explode with joy.

But the person who truly brought so much amazingness to my life was seated right at the end. Declan Davies. God, he looked good in that navy blue Oscar de la Renta sports jacket I'd picked out for him. It fit his body so beautifully. It's amazing what could happen when you actually bought clothes that were the right size.

He caught me looking at him, and his face broke out into a wide smile. He mouthed the words *I love you*, and it took every ounce of self-restraint that I had in me not to walk over to him, pick him up into my arms, and take him away. There were a million and one wicked things I wanted to do to him.

Being with Declan made me realize that throughout my life, I had approached sex in a kind of strange way. Firstly, it was the ultimate middle finger to my family who had rejected me for being gay. They might have thrown me out, but I turned that terrible experience around on its head. I found my freedom in it. I was going to be who I was—one hundred percent unapologetically me.

Secondly, I went on to treat sex like it was some sort of all-you-can-eat buffet, and my sole goal was to eat everything I possibly could. That I did. But in the same way that empty calories don't fill a person up for too long, nothing that I ever did sexually filled me up properly either.

Don't get me wrong. I had fun—a ton of it, actually—exploring all the various sides to myself and every sexual fetish ever invented. I don't regret that part of my life for a minute. But it completely paled in comparison to what I had now with Declan.

I could see, in retrospect, that the reason I was never able to find that ever-elusive fulfillment in sex was because in all the time I had spent searching for some*thing*, I was really looking for some*one*.

I just never imagined that the first time I met that someone, he would be stumbling into his office, half-drunk, after spending three days completely ignoring me.

Or that he wasn't the tough guy, big-time reporter he seemed to want the world to think that he was.

Or that despite being the most beautiful boy I had ever seen, he didn't think so and hated his body.

Or that he would look so deliciously good tied up to my bed while I was balls deep inside of him. Actually, that part I did imagine. And I couldn't stop imagining it, as my thoughts turned way too dirty for such a formal event like this.

The speaker finished, and I cleared my throat as I made my way to the podium. As the applause died down, I began my speech. Most of it was the usual fare, the standard thank yous and acknowledgements, the usual platitudes about the honor of being elected. But as I looked over at my new chief of staff, James, I slipped out a piece of paper from the inside of my jacket.

I could see his mouth gape open, but then it closed just as quickly. He'd made a joke the day before about me not adding anything else into the speech, and my expression must have given me away because he made me pinky swear not to pull any last-minute stunts on him.

But I was a Daddy Dom in my forties, and pinky swears just didn't hold the same sway that they used to. Besides, I had a feeling that once he heard what I was about to say, he wouldn't stay angry at me for long.

I had only finished this part of the speech earlier that morning, so I had to look down as I read it.

"And lastly, ladies and gentlemen, I'd like to finish on a personal note. I should warn you, though, that my chief of staff has no idea what I am about to say next, so if you see a thirty-something gentleman having a heart attack in the corner of the room, you'll know that's him."

The audience laughed, and I looked over at James. He was smiling, too—reluctantly. I continued.

"The fact that I'm even here, standing before you, is nothing short of a miracle. I am sure you are all very familiar with the story by now.

But what I'd like to talk to you about is not what has happened, but what lies before us. It's been wonderful and heartwarming to see the maturity, the grace, and the acceptance in the conversations that people have been having with each other over the last six months.

It makes us better as people, and it makes us stronger as a city. We're all different, we're all unique, but what binds us and helps us to overcome our differences is a shared understanding that we all belong. Each and every one of us.

You belong. You matter. Just as you are.

I've never felt that before in my life. In fact, I had big parts of myself that I kept hidden from the world because I didn't think that people would accept me for who I was.

But now we live in a different world. One where we are more free to be who we are, love who we love, and do what we want to do.

So I would like to share with you an insight into how my administration will be running the city. This is a new time, and as such, it calls for a new way to lead.

My administration will not be leading from the top, but instead, it will be serving you. You are the boss, and it is our job to fulfill the trust you have placed in us to make Daylesford the best city in the world.

So I encourage you to get involved in the community, in your neighborhood, and then in whatever else interests you in your life..."

A round of laughter ensued.

"Because in the words of Daylesford's favorite resident, Mrs. Langley, life's too short not to be happy."

And with that, I finished my speech as the crowd rose to their feet, giving me a standing ovation. People began milling all around me as I did the whole politician thing of shaking hands and posing for selfies.

When the crowd had finally dispersed a little, I felt a familiar firm grip on my shoulder. It was Hudson. "Great speech, my friend."

"Thanks," I said as the rest of the gang joined him.

"Yes, very much something I would expect to hear from a *governor*." Steel winked at me as he said it.

"Governor, please," Nick said in his usual loud and attitude-y way. "That sounded presidential to me. *Deffers* presidential."

Everyone laughed at that. "Guys, please, I am totally happy with where I am. But the best part of today is that I got to share it with all of you. Thank you all so much for being here. Especially Hudson and Liam, who came back just for this."

"Group hug," Mikey yelled out, and before I knew what was happening, four Daddies were being ambushed by their four boys and squished together in what appeared to be a world record attempt at the world's largest group bear hug.

After the boys finally released us from their grip, Declan came up to me. Placing his hands flat across my chest, he looked up at me and said, "I am so proud of you, Porter. You're going to be a terrific mayor."

"You're right, I am," I said as the group laughed again. "But what's going to make me really great is that I can do my job being me. I've got nothing left to hide, and it's all because of you, Declan." I planted a kiss on his sweet lips, making sure to take a gentle nibble at that lower lip of his that always drove me crazy.

"Get a dungeon, you guys," Stirling said jokingly.

I pulled myself away from Declan and looked at the man. "Not all Doms have dungeons, I'll have you know, Stirling."

"What's a dungeon?" I heard Nick ask Steel. "Is it like the nursery we have at our place?"

Steel smiled as he pressed Nick in even closer to his side. "Yeah, it's a little like that, baby."

The guys started talking amongst themselves as I turned to Steel. Once Nick had left to speak to Mikey and Liam, I leaned in toward my friend. "How are things going with you guys? Did you go to Revolver like I suggested?"

Steel shook his head. "Not yet. We have some stuff to work out."

I furrowed my brows. "Is it good stuff or bad stuff?"

Steel squinted, as if he was really thinking about it. "It's...interesting stuff. Let's leave it at that."

"No, let's *not* leave it at that," I whispered forcefully. "I may have found my boy, but that doesn't mean I've given up on liking intimate sex details from my closest friends."

Steel let out a low laugh. "Porter, you may be the most powerful man in town, but you are not getting any more information out of me."

And with that, he flashed me a toothy smile and turned away, heading over to join Nick.

"Did I just hear someone call you the most powerful man in town?" I felt Declan's question breathed into my ear.

"That's right," I said, looking over my shoulder at him. "You like that, do you?"

"Oh, Sir," he cooed, giving my lobe a blink-and-you'd-miss-it flick with his tongue. "You have no idea how much I want to be tied up and submit to the most powerful man in town."

"Right, you guys," I said, straightening up a little. The group turned to face me. "Thanks for coming, but something has, er, come up, and Declan and I need to go, and, er...resolve it."

My friends all shot me knowing looks as we quickly hugged and made our way out of there. I only had one plan for the rest of the day, and it featured Declan, tied up and underneath me.

"I love you, Porter," Declan said as we walked out of the event hand in hand.

I squeezed his fingers tightly, my lips stretched in the widest smile of my life.

"I love you too, Declan."

And I knew, beyond a shadow of a doubt, that I would love this boy with all my heart for the rest of my life.

THE END